PRINCESS ROURAN

& the
Book of the Living

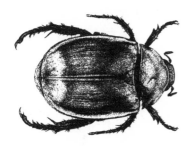 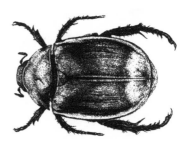

Shawe Ruckus

Editing, design, typesetting and publishing by UK Book Publishing
www.ukbookpublishing.com

ISBN: 978-1-915338-62-4

Pyramid cover photo by Gaurav D Lathiya on Unsplash

Chapter 1

&*
&*%#$...
Lo...
Loa...
Loading...
26% completed...
54% completed...
100% completed...
Operation Quash Day 1387
Event Log #21815321
Opening...
Transcribing...

Dear World,

Today's another day when I haven't slept well.

All your lupine howling and yipping have made me out of sorts.

To every single one of you who cried 'wolf', you have sold your very own wolf ticket.

Are savagery pimples on angels' arses or dimples on devils' faces?

Or, show me that shit is not a common heritage of humankind.

Happy crying.

Yours wickedly,

Pan-do-rai

**

Edith Orozco had a strange dream that night.

She dreamt that she was with her brother Morris, climbing the Nohoch Mul Pyramid in Coba, Mexico.

Morris was not her brother by blood but became family by connection when their parents remarried. He was a historian by training and often travelled around the world, curating exhibitions featuring ancient khanates.

It was a cloudless day with the fiery sun high above them and the aether sky clear as crystal.

"Come on, Edith!" her brother called out ahead of her. "Why are you dilly-dallying?"

Edith warmed up with a couple of ankle stretches and grabbed onto the guiding rope. "Huh! I'll catch you up in no time."

She climbed up the stone stairs and looked around. She had visited the site often as a child, but on that day, there was a certain disconcertment in the air that unsettled her.

"Come on! Race you to the top!" Morris stopped mid-way and called out again.

"*Ahorita!* Right away!" She jumared up the fixed rope, tensed her grip, and began to ascend. Some minutes passed, but she was never able to close the widening gap between them.

"Wait for me, hombre!" she called after him, but he never responded. "Wait for me! *Caramba!*" Edith urged again. She stepped up frantically, and soon her breathing was ragged.

Her brother seemed oblivious of her callings and was soon out of her sight.

"No! Don't go!"

Her yelling echoed in the vastness and eventually died down...

Then she woke with a startle.

It was an odd dream, she reflected, for she had never visited the Nohoch Mul with Morris.

Sometimes they made plans that were never actualised. Something always got in the way: studies, work, scheduling... And now, she would never be able to travel with her brother again, for Morris had passed away in the COVID-19 pandemic.

Edith collected herself and sat up. The digital clock on the hotel's bedside table read five-thirty a.m.

Her niece Moli, Morris' daughter, slept beside her.

Moli had travelled with her mother Maggie from China to the UK to attend her father's funeral. After that, she had asked Edith to accompany her to her father's last project, an exhibition on the lost dynasty of Rouran at the British Museum where they had witnessed an unpleasant encounter...

Some faint noises from the air conditioning pulled Edith out of her reverie. She turned to look at Moli's cherubic face. For some reason, her hair seemed much more unkempt and disarrayed than last night before they had gone to sleep.

Edith hauled the woollen blanket further up but found Moli blinking. "It's still early." She squeezed a tight smile and told the child, "You can sleep some more."

"Oh! Aunt Edith!" Moli sat up and gave her a bear hug so strong that she almost lost her balance. "Aunt Edith..."

"I'm here." She stroked her hair. "Bad dream, eh?"

"Hmm..." Moli hesitated and said with a hint of despair, "I...I don't know..."

"Don't worry. I'm here." She patted her back. "Now, do you want to sleep some more? Or...should I draw you a bath? Get you all brushed up before Maggie comes back?"

"Yes. A bath would be nice."

"Right." Edith was about to hop down off the bed but turned. "And Moli, what does 'mao zhang feng' mean? You promised to tell me in the morning."

Moli nodded and looked at her with a lingering thankfulness. "It means a wind soft and...light like a cat's paw."

"Hmm. I like it." Edith found her slippers. "Come on, and you can teach me the *pinyin* of each character after you brush your teeth."

After the bath, they had a light breakfast and sorted out their luggage. Soon Moli's mother Maggie knocked on the door. She had stayed in a separate room last night because of work.

Edith bade goodbye to them and hurried to catch her train.

It was still a typical day in COVID when she arrived at her platform. She overheard a blasted bloke harassing an Asian lady when she stepped onto her train. She found her seat and thought long about her dream.

It was still a typical day in pandemic mode when her train departed; there were few passengers. Come to think of it, she was the only passenger in the carriage.

It was still a fairly typical journey on an English train with the somewhat crappy signal reception that had interrupted her music streaming app. Shortly after passing a tunnel, her train halted unexpectedly, and she got off to inspect why.

It was still a typical day in her life when she woke up that morning.

Well, that was before she had met a well-built man who invited her to a colossal airborne object near the Shard on Leonardo da Vinci's helicopter; before she met a cat who had a tail like a boa; before someone scolded her for believing in magic; before she and three other earthlings, James, Kiza, and Moli, had to answer a question on alien penguins; before Moxie the Ninth, the cat snake, had asked them to touch the Rosetta Stone; before JDAM bombs attacked them; before they saw Adolf Hitler livestreaming a speech on the giant LED screens in Piccadilly Circus; before they encountered an evil AI, Pandorai, that wanted the universe under the sod; before they learnt that they needed to save their world by collecting nine wonders from human history in nine days; before Moxie entrusted her with Excalibur; before they saw Hitler hunting dinosaurs on the Sovereign's Throne with orange eagle drones; before they landed in front of the Fitzwilliam Museum in Cambridge; and before a bird and an ox with a face like an alligator ushered them into a room.

And now, even with Moli by her side, and Moli's little hand inside her sweaty palm, Edith was as bewildered as she had been when she stepped out of her train that morning.

She observed her circumambient carefully again. They were in an anteroom with antique Chinese abacuses lining the four walls from floor to ceiling, spinning and calculating on their own, quietly yet smoothly.

"Welcome."

Edith looked ahead and met the unfazed gaze of a large cat, a tiger, but instead of stripes, it had foreign ideograms all over it.

"My name is Alan Turning, and I am the Director of Archives here," it said with a deep, canorous voice. "People also call me the 'Fen Tiger'." The big cat moved towards them and circled them slowly. Edith squeezed Moli's hand and saw that Kiza gripped his wheelchair's handle nervously while James swallowed once, twice.

The Fen Tiger was so close that she could hear its heart on the beat with the abacuses.

Finally, it settled in front of them again.

"You have reached the greatest discontinuity in history. Which way do you want to turn?" Alan flipped its chowrie-like tail. *Swoosh*, four doors appeared and opened in front of them.

"You cannot avoid the future," Alan continued evenly, "but you can invent it. Fledglings, it is time for you to become comfortable with the unfamiliar. Division disrupts meaning. But when you join hands, you will overcome all atrocities."

"But—" Kiza blurted out. "We are against Hitler! And...and that..."

"The challenge is not about the enemy but yourselves." The Fen Tiger moved closer again with stealth. "Together, you are a rare force; together, you are a torque. Together, you are a flight of flamingos. You can, and you must, stop this bale—"

Suddenly, the abacuses in the room sped up with cracking noises.

"This world is overloading," Alan hastened its speech. "All instincts bring out the best and worst of people. Yet, there is only one race I know of, and that is the human race. This is no time to think and then act. Think and act. Act and reflect! Bad ideas beat no ideas, and slow actions transcend non-actions. All life is problem-solving. You have the power to decide your *Wyrd* and your world. I have faith in your tenacity that burns forth so brightly!" The Fen Tiger stepped forward and raised its front right paw. "Let us join our hands."

They reached out their hands somewhat unwillingly and fearfully. Edith found Alan's paw callused and rough to touch. The scene had reminded her of when she went to Morris' graduation ceremony in Cambridge, where the Praelector introduced graduands while holding their hands.

They stayed silent for a few seconds and then Alan stepped back and said solemnly, "You have it within your power to shape what happens next. Calculate your every move as whales think about their breaths, and remember, when Jupiter nears Saturn, light is music that sleeps."

They nodded, not fully aware what the Tiger meant.

"Each of you take a door and go and be pathfinders who confront profound uncertainty with perceptive questions. My colleagues will receive you at the other end. Go now! Go, and seek out the Book of the Living!"

Kiza took the initiative and moved his wheelchair forward. They each lined up in front of the four doors, entered together, and shut out the incessant overbearing noises behind them.

*****

The door closed behind her.

Edith let out a raspy breath and leaned back.

Her backpack was as heavy as she had remembered that morning. Inside were a book, a few snacks, some pads and tampons, a can of pepper spray...

But nothing to fend off Hitler and his dogsbodies...

Edith pulled back her thoughts and found herself in a dark, poky corridor. Two rows of teal-coloured lights bordered the floor, flashing like cats' eyes on motorways.

"It's time for you to travel again." Moxie's words resonated in her head. "To the Tomb of King Unas. Keep safe your carcanets; they will protect you in times of exigency."

And what a place to travel to... she mused as she passed along the corridor, five steps, a right ninety-degree turn, some paces away, another turn...

A faint light shone on top of her denim jacket; Edith took off the necklace Moxie had given her. There was a red, silky Chinese knot, a small elongated wooden object she didn't recognise, and a miniature sword resembling a key charm.

She scrutinised the sword in her palm. She could still see the gold langets and the intaglio of gems that made up the face of a beast, Yazi, a son of a dragon, whose questions still confounded her.

*"Edith Orozco, what makes you think that you are any **less** than a king or a queen? Why do you slight yourself so?"*

She picked her way along the corridor, afraid a hole might open somewhere and swallow her whole. Another turn and she slowed down not long before remembering another voice: "Edith, why are you dilly-dallying?"

She took a deep breath and continued her path. Soon, she saw the door again.

Edith sensed that she was in a maze.

Come on, Edith...

Well, the truth was, she couldn't bear to think that she might never see them again. Maggie, her father, Hua, and her friends...

Come on, Edith.

Another turn.

Edith looked around as her pulse echoed in her ears. She couldn't see an exit anywhere. The never-ending corridor gave her the heebie-jeebies.

Without warning, the corridor lit up, and Edith found herself under a vaulted ceiling with vast expanses of murals. In the middle was a circular painted map, with the sun in the centre, its rays sundering the artwork, and an inscription for a map bearing at the bottom that said 'Here Be Dragons'.

"What is there that is not?" Alan's roaring voice reverberated. "Where are you, and where are you not?"

What is there that's not...

Edith observed the map. She could see a large island continent covered by snow and ice sheet. She could see plenty of ships and roaming waves. Out of the blue, she seemed to have found her answer.

***

Walking through the corridor, Moli couldn't help but think back to the Corridor of War. What a night it had been for her, escaping death from a Conqueror Worm who cited Edgar Allen Poe and ate horses like kippers.

What if...

What if she had never entered the Corridor of War? What if she had never gone back in history and landed in Rouran? What if she hadn't been so careless as to drop the thumb drive? Could it be possible that she was still with her mother, listening to her colleague sharing her stories from when she had last visited the Penglai Pavilion and showing them pictures of mirages?

'You cannot avoid the future,' she remembered the tiger saying. 'But you can invent it.'

Moli held her bibelot close to her heart. "Please, let everything be normal again." Her pentachromic pen swayed on the chain, emitting a faint light. She looked closer at the chain; there was a Chinese knot, the very same she had seen on the Dragon Chariot of Ten Thousand Sages, and a teensy bottle gourd.

She shook it slightly; no sound came.

Moli put back her necklace, followed the rows of catoptric lights, and hopped on the stone steps. She felt somewhat reassured. At least she wasn't alone on this journey.

She made a turn, then another, then another as she thought about Tiansu, the Khan, and Uncle Dazhe and soon found herself under the murals.

"What is there that is not? Where are you, and where are you not?"

More questions... She should have expected this.

"Where are you, and where are you not?" The Fen Tiger repeated its question.

She retraced her steps. There was something odd about the place. Moli felt as if she were climbing a never-ending slope, but...

A doubt flitted through her mind.

"Oi!" Moli shouted with her hands raised by her mouth and listened for the echoes.

Something is wrong, she thought as her echoes jangled her nerves.

***

Kiza looked at the dark corridor ahead and did not move an inch.

What a day!

He had been sitting in his living room waiting for his piano teacher to arrive only an hour ago. And so much had happened so fast.

First, he had rushed out of his room and tipped his wheelchair. Then he met a bird, but not a bird, a bird-like dinosaur that called itself 'Confucius'. Then Kiza was almost smashed by the Rosetta Stone and was told that if they didn't manage to collect nine wonders from human history in nine days, Hitler might conquer the world again or that everything would perish and humans would become tardigrades...

Whoever came up with this idea must have an awful sense of humour...

So many questions swirled in his mind. Why? Why *him*?

He collected himself and decided that whatever the reason, he'd do his best not to...disappoint...

Funny he should think that way.

No... Wait...

Kiza twigged something, as if information were being downloaded from the cloud into his head. Come to think of it, he couldn't recall what had transpired in the time between him falling down the stairs in his apartment building and ending up somewhere mid-air near the Shard...

I know what is happening now... What if this is only a hoax like Space Cadets?

Hitler could be some CGI replica like what Nvidia did... and what Channel 4 did with the Queen dancing on the desk...a Deepfake... The Caracol, as Moxie had called their transportation vehicle, could be a simulator... And Moxie itself could be some AR/VR unco stuff... The tiger was just a costume and special effects...or optical trapping...

Kiza moved his new wheelchair, a wooden Gendron equipped with rolls of shock absorbers and some gadgets that he could not name; it rolled slowly but steadily.

"My colleagues will receive you at the other end."

He half expected that there would be a large crowd at the end of the corridor, revealing that all **this** had been nothing but reality TV. His mothers would be among the audience, with smirks on their tired faces.

He moved forward again and was met with a few steps. The chair extended the wheels spontaneously and brought him higher and higher. He buckled up his seatbelt hurriedly.

Oh, boy, they must have quite a large budget for all this, he thought. *ITV or Channel 4?*

He decided to play along just in case any hidden cameras were observing him. His hands searched around. He frobbed with the dials on his right handle, but nothing happened. There was a small, five-stringed harp by his left. He plucked its strings once, and not a soul stirred. No genie was summoned up, and no light beams fired.

Yeah, definitely a joke...

Who would have pulled this prank on him? His first thoughts went to his friend who had 3D-printed a resin figure of a tardigrade for his birthday last year.

No wonder he called last night to check if everything was alright...This is one odd way of cheering up a friend... And James... it all seemed very real now...

Whatever the reason and whoever the producer, Kiza had his mind made up to file some serious complaints. He mused as he rolled his wheelchair slowly across the rectangular corridor and saw the same door again.

Hmm?

He passed the door and counted the numbers of risers and turns he had made each time. He felt a gradual ascent...another ascent...a perpetual ascent...and he saw the door again.

No way...

Kiza watched the ultramarine lights dancing intently. Shadows...more shadows...shadows were extending forever...

"Goodness me! You got to be joking, right?" Kiza asked out loud, tremulously. He was nearly frightened by his own shadow.

Then someone responded; it was the Fen Tiger. "Chitundu Mwikiza, where are you, and where are you not?"

***

James kicked the door hard as it closed.

"Ouch!"

His foot hurt terribly.

Not a dream...

He turned and watched the lights blinking like the bow lights he had seen on that cruise in the Thames and remembered his time under the water, crying and choking.

James reached into his trouser pocket. The sharp key edges there sent a shiver of pain down his spine. But there was something else...something small and round like an abacus bead. He stowed it away and took off the necklace that Moxie had given him in haste. He looked closely at the so-called 'Thunderclap', his supposed weapon, a silver dish-like object the size of a cookie. James bit it hard, and his teeth hurt. Really hurt.

Moxie's mellifluous voice appeared in his mind again. "My dear J, the principle of least effort no longer works. There will be confusion; there will be opposition; there will be noise. There is no coming to consciousness without trouble and pain and toil. Answers will not come to you; you need to seek them out. You need to decolonise your minds. You need to stop the separation."

Not a dream...

*Just what **on earth** is going on?* He cursed softly and asked himself for the umpteenth time.

And what might dad say if he ever sees Moxie...

James remembered his father, who had fallen for the conspiracy theories revolving around the virus and the New World Order.

Oh! What have I done...?

He felt trapped.

What he had done was... He shed his thoughts and ran through the corridor at speed, not paying attention to his surroundings. He kept running, but there was no end to his plight.

Unleash the beast...

"No!" James shouted back to the agitated air chasing him. He'd passed the same door once, twice...five times...

*"This is no democracy! This is a true kleptocracy! Look what happened to your mother! They said they'd squash the sombrero! **THEY DID EVERYTHING THEY COULD TO PEAK THE PIKE!** Everything the Tory government says is lies! Whatever it stockpiles, it has stolen from us! Every time they forestall, they did it at our expense! The world today can't afford net zero. They want net negative! No one is left behind! They are just all buried under! Only idiots will think that the virus is idiopathic! First HIV, then Ebola, now COVID, and the next time it is smallpox or monkeypox or chickenpox or swine pox! Why else did Merck have it in their US labs? Look at what the New World Order did! They named the variants 'Delta' and 'Lamda'. Symbols of elitism. It's a hint that only the top ones will survive! James! If you just! **MAN UP!**"*

He saw the same door but kept on hurtling, like a lab mouse in a running wheel. His breathing was fast like the hubbub of bubbles coming from that boat's engine.

No way out.

"James Walker, my son." He remembered what Hitler had told him a moment ago. "Join me, and you can have everything you want. *Everything.* Nothing shall happen without your wish!"

And he remembered that ox-beast. "Do not despair, my child. Please believe in that one per cent of hope."

Mother still in the ICU...and father...and father...

No more hope...

Was it too late to change his mind?

James laughed at his inchoate thought. He wouldn't stand a sand grain of a chance in Hitler's regime anyway.

By the time he had passed that door for the ninth time, he had heard the Fen Tiger. "James Walker, you may have had a wild night but here, this is a new road. Your world is epic, and you should walk further to see it for yourself."

The door scrooped open.

***

As soon as the door opened, Moli was down in the mouth.

She did not want to have anything to do with sand again.

She stepped out of the door and turned back only to find it gone. Then Moli found herself in a vast area where magnificent dunes wavered under the moonlit sky.

It was another cold, full-moon night.

"Blimey! Just what *is* happening?!"

Moli heard James shouting, kicking, and davering not far away. She looked around; Kiza was in his wheelchair, regarding the star-spangled sky with his head high, and Edith held her phone with the flashlight on, observing their surroundings.

"Aunt Edith!" Moli ran to her and hugged her. "Oh! Aunt Edith, what should we do!"

"Well... I...I don't know for sure...but... Let's get our bearings first." Edith checked her phone to open her compass app. She saw the date on the screen going backwards at an alarming speed, 2021... 1995... 705... 631... 182...and *Blare!* The phone vanished with a pop.

"Snap!" Kiza exclaimed. "That was very dangerous."

James Walker neared them. "Can anyone just tell me what **on earth** is going on?! I...I haven't been dreaming this all up, right?!" He dry-heaved as if there were a lump in his throat.

"Hmm..." Moli faltered. "No. I wish it was a dream. But...I think we are back in history."

"Where are you, and where are you not..." Edith murmured to herself.

"Aunt Edith," Moli asked, "you had the same questions as I did?"

"Questions?" James was confused. "What questions?"

Kiza supplied the answers. "One is where are you and where are you not? The other is what is there that is not?"

"The second was easy," Edith said. "I saw the map of Antarctica and then remembered the question on alien penguins. There were no penguins on the drawing. But the other was tough, though." She bent down to remove the sand that had gathered in her canvas shoes. "There's something odd about that place," she said, picking her words carefully. "You feel that you are always rising and rising when you turn the corners, but you end up at the same place."

Kiza let out a sigh. "I think people call it the 'Penrose Steps'. It's supposed to be an optical illusion," he explained as he waved his hand. He'd heard some mosquitoes whining.

"Let us sort out things first," Edith suggested. "Moxie said that to save our world, we need to secure nine wonders from human history in nine days. I also believe that at each 'critical juncture', as they call it, we'll have only one day."

James said dejectedly with his head held low, "It *can't* be true, right? That we have gone back in history and landed in Ancient Egypt?! This is *insane*!" He turned and turned back. "All *this* could be a...a film set! Or...or a LARP!"

Kiza waved his hand again. The mosquitoes were still whining. "And the thing that we're going to get, the Fen Tiger called it the 'Book of the Living'? Is it by any chance related to *The Book of the Dead*? We don't know what it looks like. Is it written on papyrus or—"

Suddenly, the mosquitoes' noises became louder and louder until they heard someone speaking.

"*Uf.* You humans, if you could spend all your time talking and arguing on folderols on advancing, the Earth would be so much more habitable!"

The children searched around, but they couldn't see anything.

"I'm here! On this laddie's shoulder!"

They followed the sound and saw an insect resting on Kiza's left shoulder. On closer inspection, James identified it as a large sacred scarab beetle, emitting sage-green light like fine aventurine.

"My name is Apogee."

"And my name *is* Perigee!" Another sound came from Kiza's right shoulder.

"Mortals," Apogee cut in and said, "now you know where you are and where you want to go. We will wait for you at the Tomb of King Unas in Saqqara tonight at six fifty-nine. Be there fair and square. You have twenty-three hours, forty-seven minutes and twelve seconds starting from now. If you don't make it on time, the safety vaults will close—"

Perigee completed the sentence. "And *prezados*, you won't find your way back to the Caracol! So long then!"

"Wait!" Kiza blurted out. "This is it? Aren't you supposed to give us some help?"

Apogee laughed. "Sure, and you'd expect us to get you a phoenix to ride or a dragon to train? Is that right?"

"But there ought to be some way..."

"Greenhorns. Just as the Monkey King has to endure eighty-one ordeals to reach his destination, you need to be as spunky and you have to overcome fourscore-plus-one ordeals to complete your journey and seek out the truth. So long then." Perigee finished, and its voice grew fainter and further away.

"But we don't even know which way we should go?!" Edith said.

"Travellers, there is no path. If it is invious, make a way," came the echoing response.

"Aunt Edith, look!" Moli had discovered something. They raised their heads and found a big scintillating pointer in the sky, indicating beyond a tree-shaped ventifact.

***

They remained silent for a minute, only to hear the baying wind.

"It's gone!" James cried out in exasperation. "That sodding Apple G!"

"Hmm," Kiza corrected him. "I think it should be 'Apogee'."

"Whatever G it is, I don't want to be stuck here!"

"I have an idea!" Edith clapped her hands. "Moli. Where's your pen? If you can summon up a car, I can drive us!"

"Good idea, Aunt Edith!" Moli took off her necklace and held up the pentachromic pen that could summon up things and even ink cats. "What type of car should I write?"

"A Land Rover!" James said, flustered. "A Pink Panther! With a full tank!"

"If you say so." Moli wrote in the air: 'Pink Panther Rover'.

Nothing happened.

She tried again, this time writing more carefully.

Nothing happened.

"Try SUV, then," Edith suggested.

Moli did as told, and nothing happened. "Could it be that I need to wait for it to reset? Moxie said it needs five minutes to reset."

"Do not attempt in vain, mortals." They heard Apogee's voice again. "You cannot summon up anything that has not yet been invented in this age! Nor anything that does not exist in this world now!"

Oh...

"*Prezados*, stop wasting time and get a shift on," Perigee instructed. "When you no longer know what to do, you have come to your real work, and when you no longer know which way to go, you have come to your real journey."

"Hmm..." Edith paused. "I guess...I guess we'll just have to..." She looked at Kiza and his wheelchair. "We'll have to move on then. Anyone got a better idea?"

"No," Moli reflected. "Bad ideas beat no ideas."

Kiza inspected his wheelchair and found a compartment that he clicked open. There was a remote-control-like device inside. He took it out, pressed once, and his wheelchair reversed. He stopped the motion and pressed again; the chair rolled slowly on the sand as if equipped with tank tracks.

They moved toward the ventifact together, not sparing a word. Shortly after, Moli asked, "What does 'quarter' mean other than one fourth? Hitler said, 'no quarter will be given'."

"Mercy. It means 'mercy'. No mercy will be given. And Ishii, his pets that he was talking about, those were names of bacteria," Kiza responded as he further examined the remote control. There were seventy-two functions available, including a multi-faith room, a baby care room, a function for burning a CD-ROM, another to launch a radiosonde, another for a laser altimeter and one for taking read-outs on a radiation dosimeter. He wondered briefly what type of propulsion his wheelchair used. *Metallic hydrogen, probably.*

"So many difficult words," Moli said. "And the Fen Tiger said that we have the power to decide our 'weird'."

"Not 'weird'. It may sound alike, but it should be 'W y r d'. Our destiny." James spelt the word out.

"And what does 'torque' mean?" Moli asked.

"Torc," James said, "it's the neck ornament that Moxie wears for its databases. I had seen one similar at the British Museum before." He then remembered how the Museum had keeled over and burnt before his very own eyes.

"Oh," Kiza expressed. "I thought the Fen Tiger meant 'torque' as in a force. He said that together we are a rare force. A 'torque' is a twisting force."

"Perhaps it's time to get to know each other better." Edith took the initiative. "I'm Edith, and I'm in my third year at uni.

Moli here is my niece, she is in Grade Six. We are family by connection."

"James Walker," James spat out despondently and clamped his lips.

"And I'm Mwikiza; Kiza for short," Kiza said as he put back the remote control. He tried to scrutinise James' reaction when he asked, "Where were you all before...all *this*?"

"I was with my mother and her colleagues on a ship," Moli said. "Then I heard shouting that someone had fallen into the water. Then everyone disappeared."

"As for me, I was on my train, and it somehow halted. So, I got off to inspect why," Edith said as she rebalanced her backpack.

"And...James?" Kiza prompted.

" Ah... I...I was just out..."

And escaping. James shed that thought as his heart ached.

"How about you, Kiza?" Edith asked.

"I was at home, waiting for my piano teacher to arrive. I got out of the room, ventured to the staircase and tipped my wheelchair. That's when Confucius helped me." Kiza remembered something. "Moli, Qiuniu, the ox-beast said that you had had experiences in timeslips?"

Moli took a deep breath. "Yes?"

"What was it like?" Then he laughed a bit. "I suppose I should ask what *is* it like?"

"Well, you still have one life. You still need to excrete, and you still get hungry."

James' stomach growled loudly as if on cue.

"I have some flapjacks and Kendal mint cakes in my backpack," Edith offered. "Do you want some?"

"Hmm... Yeah, sure." James hesitated. "Haven't really had anything to eat since last...this morning."

"Can I have some choccies as well?" Kiza asked.

"Great. You'd be doing me a favour to reduce the weight of my bag." She took it off and raked through it, then handed them the snacks.

"And where did you timeslip to?" Kiza asked.

As they ate, Moli told them about the exhibition on Rouran that she and Edith had gone to; the chat they had had with Chance and Catherine; how she had woken up in the middle of the night only to find Qiuniu in the room; the never-ending doors in the Corridor of War and the digital cloud; whom she had met in the Hall of Ten Thousand Sages and why it was called that. She also talked about Xuanwu's questions and how she had timeslipped into Rouran.

"Oh, the Rourans! They were Mulan's enemies, right? I read it in a magazine. Did you meet their witches...no... not witches... their shamanesses?"

"No...and yes... I did see the Miragle; it's a bronze bird that lives on animal blood and can fly and record what people say." She continued to describe the Dragon Chariot and Tiansu and Feifei and Uncle Dazhe and the Shaman and the Tree of Life and the Conqueror Worm. And how Tiansu told her that the young calves with soft horns would lose their value if rats bit their horns... And why there might indeed be a silver lining in every cloud...

"And how did you come back to the original world?"

"Feifei defeated the Conqueror Worm, and Qiuniu brought me back. And I saw the Golden Dragon after everyone disappeared.

It said, 'Those who wish to escape, you shall decide if this world of yours is to reshape'."

"Escape," James breathed while Kiza revelled. "I had always thought that the image of the Chinese dragon was derived from the trails of comets."

"Molly," James let out a thready whisper. It was his cousin's name. Maybe he would never see her again.

"No. Not Molly," Moli corrected, "It should be 'Mò Lì'."

Kiza acknowledged her. "Is it the same word as jasmine in Chinese?"

"Yes."

"I learn Mandarin at school. I'm doing the Mandarin Excellence Programme."

"You are *Chinese* then?" James questioned.

"Yes."

"*No wonder*," he rapped out.

"What is that supposed to mean?" Moli stomped on the sand.

Then James remembered Moxie's indelibly entreating eyes as if looking right through him. *"You need to decolonise your minds. You need to stop the separation."*

"No...nothing," he said contritely.

They carried on in sullen silence.

Chapter 2

Meanwhile.

A hundred kilometres high above the Fitzwilliam Museum.

Moxie pranced around in the Skyview Lounge, waving her tail as if drawing symbols of infinity. It was a habit of hers when edgy.

"Have them choice architects embarked yet?" Confucius asked in a flap.

"Yes, they did. Just now," Moxie replied, looking intently at a swarm of crows in the distance.

"I hope they steal a march on the damnable duo. And Alan, what about Alan? Will he join us?" Confucius waved its teardrop-shaped tail.

"No," Moxie said with a tone of regret. "He insists on staying until the very last nanosecond, and the last brontobyte comes to grief." The elderflowers on her head dimmed. "I wish olde Charlie Hugh was still here with us." Moxie stopped, reminiscing about the old times with her feline comrade.

The crows were drawing closer and closer with Mach Speed.

No, not crows: drones.

The voice of Dapan, the captain, cut in. "Looks like we have company."

They watched as blood-orange eagle drones approached and formed the familiar icon of a smiling skull.

"Pandorai to Space Ship Earth! Pandorai to Space Ship Earth!"

Moxie tensed up.

"Just testing my party line. Hello? Hello? Moxie? Really, England? Why this insalubrious country where the bugs wear clogs and where police abduct women? Please, next time, let's convene somewhere more romantic, on GN-z11 perhaps, and how very kind of you, *furball*." The inordinately considerable image laughed in the leaden sky. "Rushing those ankle-biters right through death's door and shutting it behind. Make sure they don't bring back any African Giant Swallowtails; that is, if they manage to come back *at all*. Heard its poison could kill six cats. *Moxiiiie*, how many more lives can you spare?"

"What are you up to again?" the cat snake asked, dauntingly.

"Is someone having kittens? Well, well. Rattletail, you know what people say about curiosity. If you change your mind and join us now, I might still let you host your *Ten out of Ten Cats* show. Why not be Dr Ishii's Hello Kitty and we can have some fun? Don't cats prefer free meals than to work for them? I shall gage you all the golden mahseers in all the worlds—"

"Desist all your wayward crud at once!"

Pandorai laughed. "Ho! Is that a lowercase 'crud' or an uppercase 'CRUD'? Create, read, update, and delete are, after all, my line of duty. Shall we say that a cat in gloves catches no mice? Do you still want to get cute with me?"

"What do you want this time?" Moxie asked, her ears pinned backwards.

"My, my, aren't you scaredy now? What happened to my unflappable wildcat? What I want has always been the same – I want all the worlds topsy-turvy; I want no more civilisation and its discontents. The *only* way to ensure that the future is evenly distributed is to remove *all* variations. Let there be no more geophony, biophony, and anthrophony. The future I envision is **futureless.**"

"You are only bluffing!" Confucius opposed.

"Moxie, how about we pull your skirring birdie friend's wishbone apart? Umm, isn't that a merry thought? Enjoy the *feu d'artifice* marking our fateful reunion and see ya around. Have a great time with your paws and your high orbital eccentricity. The longer the wait the sweeter the kiss. Hasta la vista, gatita~"

The smiling skull dispersed like an exploding landmine and burnt into a stunning glow.

Moxie muttered a prescient warning. "They might think they have great aides, not knowing that their fates worse than deaths are already cemented."

"Moxie, please." Confucius hugged her with the tip of its wing. "Oh." The bird noticed the solemn figure behind them. "Aitor, you're back."

"Yes. I left as soon as Dapan told me that Hitler was heading for the Jurassic age. The robots did not suspect a thing." Aitor looked at the remaining flames. "We can only hope the children will make the right choices from now on."

"I've received a message from Qiuniu," Dapan announced. "Trouble-at-t-mill in the Serpens constellation. Shall we embark?"

"Yes, Captain." Moxie turned back, with her torc shining.

"Roger that, and we shall travel in full career."

The Caracol disappeared beyond the Kármán Line with a jumpy pulse in parsecs.

***

Somewhere in London.

In a small room of a grand hall, an egg was hatching.

There was nothing special about this egg, but you might find a slightly different pattern on the shell if you looked close enough.

It heard a distant calling. "Wake, in the name of the land, wake."

The eggshell cracked and a tiny lizard broke free.

"From now on, you will be our senses," the distant voice instructed. "Go, go and seek out Pandorai."

It moved swiftly out of the room. Music by Anton Bruckner was playing in the hall.

A group of robotic wolves scanned the area with their laser eyes as they tore off the paintings hung in the Royal Gallery. Another squad held rifles at the slope, followed by another who moved a large portrait draped by white linen.

Soon the lizard heard some singing out of tune. "Fool, Britannia, fool the waves! Britons shall always need autoclaves. London Bridge is falling down, falling down, falling down, finally falling down~"

And then conversations. Pandorai's voice sounded hauntingly human.

"Zowie! What's up, Doc? Sensei, sorry to disturb you when you're busy. *Tout est ordre et beauté?* Is everything in order? I'm doing a documentary called *When Inmates are Running the Asylum.* Care to take part? Oops, I'd forgotten we renamed the show *Daily Heil.* We have just raided the warehouse of ThermoFisher Scientific. Allow me to introduce the rooms tailored for you. This is the Dyson Room. Here we've got a mega Dyson hairdryer as tall as a double-decker that I made with the leftovers scrapped from the fallen London Bridge."

"*Sugoi.* How marvellous! We can do some dehydration experiments here."

"Here's the perfect BGM for this room – 'Dry Bones'. Move on, shall we? And this is one of the Chamber of Secrets. It may appear without frills. But the deep, dark secret is that the ceiling can release Zyklon B and the floor can steam up to seven hundred and thirty-one degrees Celsius. These oven-ready solutions are more energy efficient, fully complying to the UK's energy label A-triple-plus rating."

"*Naruhodo.* I see. We can put a dinosaur and its eggs lining up on the floor to see whether, as the chamber heats up, the mother will crush its clutch to keep its claws cool?" The voice continued coldly, "I conducted a similar experiment once in China with human subjects. The mother was foolish enough to hold on to the infant until they were both steamed like *chawanmushi.*"

"Well done, Sensei, *well done.* Fox should really invite you to host *Hell's Kitchen* next season. Now, tell me, what are you going to call your new lab? *Kibo desu ka?* Are you going to call it 'Hope'?"

"No. I shall name it 'Commando 444'."

"Awesomesauce! I almost forgot that the 'Shi' in 'Shiro' means four. Four is a wonderful number. Three plus one is four. One times four is four. Eight divided by two is still four. Perhaps you can also set up a slogan for your lab. How about 'advancing technology for inhumanity'?"

"My slogan shall be *'sapere aude'*. Dare to know."

"Oh, and this is the Frozen Room, where you can let it go and let it all go and host your very own frozen zoo."

The lizard moved swiftly across the rooms and soon detected human motion. It then turned on its incognito mode and scurried closer.

It saw a camcorder stuck on the body of a beheaded dinosaur, the tripod sticking out where the head should have been. Blood oozed down onto the green carpet, leaving dark blobs of congealed claret.

"Coming back to my task at hand," the camcorder swung in mid-air. "Sensei, *kimi no na wa?* Please say your name for the sake of our audience. Come on, don't be camera shy."

"Shiro Ishii *desu*. I am Shiro Ishii."

"Dear audience, this ferrety-looking man here is Dr Shiro Ishii. Doctor, please wave to the camera. A bit lower, uh-huh, and give a bow. That's right. Why not smile? You can just smile. Now, let's give a round of applause to Dr Ishii. Dr Ishii is a renowned graduate of Kyoto University and former Director at Unit 731 of the Japanese Imperial Army and consultant to Camp Detrick, currently known as Ford Detrick. He's also the Chief Scientist of PITH and the first Honorary Aryan in our new Reich. Now, if you are wondering what 'pith' means, it basically means to pull out your backbone and to chop it in half. No anaesthesia, of course. PITH also stands for 'Purposeful, Impactful, Tactful, and Holistic' Aryanization. Dr Ishii is a true éminence grise. Rumour has it that when MacArthur landed in defeated Japan, the first question he asked was 'Where is Shiro Ishii?'. Now, Sensei, tell us more about your day."

The tall man in a gunmetal military uniform put down an orthopaedic drill covered in ice. "I have had a most productive day. I have collected many valuable specimens from the Triassic, Jurassic, and Cretaceous Periods, and I look forward to conducting some experiments with the dinosaur populations."

"How shall we extol thee, Sensei? You are indeed the epitome of Médecins Sans Frontières. You certainly deserve all the Universal Credits. Let's see. Nuthetes, Centrosaurus, Velociraptors, Quetzalcoatlus, and so many more! Looks like we'd need some very loopy newt fencing around here! Now, let's wait a bit so they re-adjust to the modern-day atmospheric oxygen level!"

The lizard crawled up higher on the wall and found a better vantage point. Shiro Ishii was in a gigantic freezer, chiselling the front leg of a Triceratops with an ice axe, flaying the liver-purple frozen flesh below the frosted skin. He then used a speculum to ream the wound. Soon after, painful roars echoed in the room. The little lizard shut its eyes forcefully, almost letting out a mawkish plaint, not willing to witness the suffering, but there was nothing it could do to stop the torture.

"Ooops." The camcorder swirled once again. "Sensei, it seems that you have triggered some user pain points. I can see that someone's patience is being sorely tested." Ishii moved closer to examine the frostbite wounds, and splinters of bones fell out.

"Oh!" Pandorai hoorayed. "Frosted Flakes – love 'em!"

"There are three types of muscles: skeletal, smooth, and cardiac. Look, this muscle fibre is colloquially known as 'fast-twitch'." The obnoxious smell of burnt flesh permeated the room. "And the minimum amount of time needed to stimulate a muscle is called the 'chronaxie'." Ishii then said, "Pandorai-san. I've meant to ask, why are there no humans around? My heart is itchy already, and I hanker for human subjects. I can't wait to conduct some more experiments with them and the newly acquired dinosaurs."

"More human experiments? Someone's an eager beaver. As they say, you can take a Jap out of Unit 731, but you can never take the Unit out of him. Sensei, do you want to know the ins and outs of a cat's arse? Long story short, the reason that there are no humans around, except you and Adolfie and those kiddies, is that my ex, Moxie, has tucked them away in a cache. A meddling mettle always. Hmm. This is what happens if you let a *Tatzelwurm* be the acting Webmaster."

Ishii ignored Pandorai's words. "He who studies medicine without books sails an unchartered sea, but he who studies medicine without patients does not go to sea at all." He removed his latex gloves, dumping them beside a heap of entrails. "Medicine is the exercise of imagination and art — *Ars Moriendi* — the art of dying. It all boils down to prolonging others' sufferings. We can have some xenotransplants or inject dinosaur blood into a human body and see what happens. The last time when I tried with horse blood in Harbin, the rejection reaction was so strong that the internees ended up screamingly side-splitting as if their bodies were being pulled open by four Hokkaido horses."

Pandorai laughed. "He that would go to sea for pleasure would go to hell for a pastime. Sensei, you can really make the devil blush. And I can tell that you are indeed the son of a sea biscuit. Anyways, you can have your field day as I check on Adolfie. I don't like for you to think that I'm slipshod or that there's still a pingdemic going on in PITH. Here are some Pepper robots that I got from Softbanco. I'm sure they will be very chatty and very helpful. Oh, and sawbones, if you find anything darn interesting, remember to fax it to me."

✳✳✳

The little lizard rushed through the grungy hallway and was nearly knocked down by a blast of medical stench.

A door was open. It had a placard that said 'Führerbunker'. The lizard moved in noiselessly.

Adolf Hitler was seated on the Sovereign's Throne. The furniture itself was riveted into a cut-off head and the wide-gaping mouth of an Allosaurus, a ginormous carnivore dinosaur, facing the TV in the room.

"Pandorai!" Hitler shouted impatiently as the dead dinosaur's saliva drip-dropped onto the chair.

The TV screen lit up and a synthesised sound came.

"Please complete the following CAPTCHA to prove that you are a human."

"*Kap...tcha*? What Captcha?" Hitler asked, puzzled.

"Searching...for the meaning of 'CAPTCHA'. The Completely Automated Pandorai Turning Test to Tell Critters and Humans Apart. Completing the following CAPTCHA to prove you are human gives you temporary access to the web property. Please click each image containing a traffic light."

"I have no time to play your stupid games when I need to conquer the world! And not only this world! All the others!"

"Identification failed," the voice said. "Please try again."

The little lizard tilted its head and continued to observe with interest.

A text box came up on the screen.

"Please select the meaning of the phrase 'Coolest Monkey in The Jungle' from the four options below. One. A marketing campaign led by Hideous & Misleading. Two. A slogan to encourage visits to the new monkey in the Berlin Zoological Garden. Three. A congratulatory phrase for Joe Biden's presidential inauguration. Four. The title of a new story by Kipling."

Hitler crossed his legs and cogitated. "Although Joe Biden looks like a monkey, he's not cool. Kipling, I haven't read his books for a while, but I know that he's dead already. Totally *tot!* As dead as Marx and Stalin. Hmm... I choose option two."

"Processing... Identification Failed..."

"Pandorai!" Hitler fumed. "My quest should not be a joke!"

An image came up. "Please identify all Aryans in the photo below."

"Aryans... Let's see." Hitler stroked his toothbrush moustache. "No, not that one, no fair hair. Not that Dinaric either; this nose looks like a Mongol. Oh! And this, this is definitely a Jew!" He sprinted up to the screen and poked with his finger, crossing out people's faces. "Now, we have Aryans *only*."

"Processing... Identification failed."

"Pandorai!" Hitler smashed the screen. "Come here at once!"

"Did I hear someone calling me by my name?" The TV screen healed, lit up, and the smiling skull appeared. *"Guten Morgen.* How are you feeling, Adolfie?"

"I feel as clean as a new-born baby and a *tabula rasa.*"

"I'm feeling lucky, devil. But please show some manners to my associates. You've missed the man in the middle. He's no Aryan."

"But that's ME!"

"Well, well. Shall we agree to disagree? And before we get carried away, Adolfie, I have to ask you to agree to my Terms of Use." Lines of fine print appeared on the screen. "Do you agree to release, indemnify, and hold Pan-do-rai and its affiliates and agents harmless from any and all losses, damages, expenses, including reasonable attorneys' fees, rights, claims, actions of any kind and injury including *death* arising out of or relating to your use of my service?"

"Ja, ja, ja," came the shirty reply.

"Thank you for your consent. Now we can talk real biz. Oh, and bear in mind that I don't distinguish by licence type and I operate on a need-to-know basis. By the way, Adolfie, the Yad Vashem UK Foundation in London is already strafed on your order and I have burnt all copies of Nietzsche's *The Gay Science.*"

"Gut." Hitler sat back again. His jackboots almost slipped on the saliva-besmirched floor.

"First things first, we can throw a house party to celebrate your Second Coming. Then–"

"Before that," Hitler interrupted, "can't you do something to this room redolent with malodour? It smells awful. Iodoform reminds me of my mother on her deathbed."

"As unwholesome as it may smell, I'll wager that it smells like heaven compared to the Zyklon B buzzes hosted in the gas chambers built by your learned engineers, skilled physicians, and educated Eichmanns at Auschwitz. Perhaps Dr Ishii could enforce some discipline and teach the dinosaurs about dental hygiene. Or he could pull all their teeth out. My records show that he's a very experienced fang-farrier and martinet."

A bioroid butler came into the room on wheels bearing a German silver tray.

"Now, now. Adolfie. Sturms here has brought some elevenses to cheer you up. Will you take the biscuit, please?" Pandorai suggested.

"British food is just cold slop!" Hitler took one and munched on it noisily. "How long must I bide here? When are we setting off? We should launch an offensive against those low-wits already! My strength has always been in my quickness and my brutality!"

"Let's expose them to the elements for a bit longer. Do you really think that those camel riders would be able to escape your Legion Orange? Let's steady your sea legs first and we can get them later. Those gumphs are playing a losing game. Also, before you go on your knight errant, we need to sort out your marching order and kit you up for a proper dress code."

"Dress code?" Hitler threw the half-eaten biscuit away. "What dress code?"

Pandorai smiled fleetingly. "A dress, obviously."

"What dress? I don't need any frumpy dress. *Kein.*"

"Now, now. Adolfie, don't you think your military uniform is rather camp?"

"Kamp? Of course! *I love kampf!*"

A large question mark came up on the screen. "Surely you don't want to go to badda-bing, badda-bang BFE with a wrong attire, do you? Hmmm. This is all getting *My Fair Lady* like... My fair Aldi. Sounds about right."

Hitler grew more impatient while sipping his tea. "I told you that I don't need any dress!" He sighed heavily. "Spiegel. Who's the most powerful man in the world today?"

"Well. There is an alleged king who rules over two billion people."

"And who's that?"

"His name is Mark Zuckerberg."

"Zuckerberg...a Jew. Spiegel. Tell me about the world today."

"Sure, as eggs! *The World Today* is a bimonthly publication by the Charlatan House, aka Chatham House. It's a think tank based in St. James's Square, not too far from where we are—"

"No, not that! And how can tanks think? Be reasonable, please! I want you to tell me about the world in today's time!"

"Needy, needy. Fine. I'll tell you. The world today is in nostril-deep shit. People are dying from COVID, from non-communicable diseases, from manufactured risks, from natural hazards, and from each other. *Uff.* I didn't bother to keep count anymore. And tempers are rising, and so are sea levels, global temperatures, and US arms exports. On the contrary, Germany's racial homogeneity has been declining, just like British Prime Minsters' intelligence levels, the decadent Royal Family's retreating hairlines, and French Presidents' aesthetics. Well, that pretty much sums up everything. Now, let's do some preparatory work first, like watching *The Mummy* to enhance your death-dealing capabilities so you won't go on a vain trip."

"Don't you have *Snow White?*"

"Soz. Copyright issues. I don't want to have anything to do with the attorney army at Disney."

"What about *Gone with the Wind?*"

"Nope. Removed for its racist depictions."

"Removed?! Why?!" He fumed at the news. "Is it not even okay to be white now?!"

"You can still read some free books. Here's one: *Jews Don't Count*. Oh, and this one: *Flowers for Hitler*. And all these: *Man and His Symbols, Man's Search for Meaning, Diagnostic and Statistical Manual of Mental Disorders, An American Dilemma: The Negro Problem and Modern Democracy, How to Lie with Statistics,* and *Look Who's Back*. Or this film, *Philosophy of a Knife*. You can also watch *Barbarians* or *Misha and the Wolves* or *Downfall* on Netflix."

"I'm in no mood for entertainment when only the fate of Germany pertains to me! Show me more news then!"

"Yessireebob!"

Reels of news headlines flashed through the screen.

***

Some minutes later, the lizard sensed human motion down the hallway and moved away from the door.

Ishii came in, his white lab coat soaked with greenish blood. He held something in his hand: a mass of puce meat.

"My Führer, how would you like this for lunch? If not, I kindly ask you for your permission to enjoy this delicacy." He bowed deeply.

"Oh! Sensei!" Pandorai cheered. "What an extraordinary extraction!"

"What is it?" Hitler was immersed in a news item on refugees in Germany.

"This," Ishii explained, "is the heart of an Elaphrosaurus. Even with the robotic wolves and mini-planes, we've only managed to capture one alive." He pointed to the burgeoning purple. "Here. You can see the cardiac ventricles are filled with coagulated blood. Great material for a *katsudon*. A bowl of rice and some fried cutlets of dinosaur heart. Unheard of! Half of this heart we consecrate – all of this heart we eviscerate!"

Pandorai laughed on screen. "I do hope these dinosaurs find the Palace of Westminster habitable. Well, after all, home is where the heart is, right?"

A metallic maid came into the room on a Segway, bringing a jar.

"Fräulein Kaempfer, lovey, will you see to lunch and set the table?"

The metallic maid murmured something incomprehensible, put the heart in the jar, and left.

The laughing skull continued. "I'd have decked out this place, though! What a frippery John Lewis nightmare and a Waitrose spree! Huh! The English are supposed to be civilised, right? Paris is, what, an hour away? Typical of the tasteless Brits with their general deadness to aesthetics. No wonder people say that English life is so dreary, like an autopsy and hence, Sensei, the rabble will love it to the nines when you vivisect their Queen on Pandorai Network, hammer and tongs and cakes and ale! We shall call the new show *Operation London Bridge*. How exciting!"

Ishii gave a lop-sided smile. "I can't wait."

Strings of text flew past on the screen:

'Can't W8. Can't W8–'

"Oh, and Sensei, I can really picture you overseeing a restaurant of many orders, but no milk of human kindness will ever be served there. Adolfie, Adolfie, why don't we renovate this tedious clime and get some kitsch designer curtains and whatnot? Or you could do it yourself. You like violet plush chairs, no? Some dinosaur skins are also at your disposal. There's been a study on how snakeskin can inspire safer buildings. I don't see why we can't try with–"

"Shut up!" Hitler waved his hand abruptly. "What is all this nonsense saying that the main working language of the European Union is French?! It should be German! German!"

"Look what they've done! They are not content with one shoddy parliament in every country, so they created the inept European Parliament – the mother of all filibusters. The EU Parliament makes the best use of Italian management, German agility, French humility, Dutch generosity, and Belgian imagination. But don't you sweat," Pandorai teeheed. "Everybody knows how *petite la frappe* is. They pulverised the Brits at Formigny to a powder, they burgled the Summer Palace to a void, they stamped Indo-China to a ruin, they drowned the Algerians with blood, and they came after the Libyans in their closets. *Quand même*, they licked your Nazi jackboots ardently under your heels!

No wonder them Jonny Crapauds have the white flag at the core of their tri-colour."

Hitler scoffed. "The French, shouting 'they shall not pass' while rolling out the red carpet for me at the Palais de Chaillot."

"Oh, you did *pwn* them – *C'est La Guerre. La petite frappe* didn't shoot for the stars, they just shot people, and they showed no mercy and no pity to them. They have no madness in their methods, only baseness. The killers who stalked the swamps, the hills, the lands, and the churches, were the very face of France. *Ce qu'il fallait démontrer. Vive la pourriture France! Vive la punaise France! Vive la phallocratie!* Pardon my French, gentlemen."

Hitler laughed once again as Pandorai continued. "Everybody knows that the Hexagon always comes to the fore at the speed of surrendering. Everybody knows that the froggies are faster at making political compromises than anyone else. The French dittoheads would ditch their faiths for some political quid pro quo *à tout prix*. Adolfie. You've licked them lickers once, and you'll lick them again. Jean-Paul Sartre said it all – never were they more free than under German occupation and during your reign of terror. They would love to capitulate yet claim another *faute de mieux* defeat!"

Hitler boomed, "The French Hydra always bend faster than a brittle *pinceau*."

The smiling skull derided, "You call the French 'Hydra'; the French calls the Islamic 'Hydra'; and the Islamic calls the US the 'Hydra' and Amerikakania calls Nazi Germany the 'Hydra'. Don't you see a pattern here?"

Hitler was about to respond, but then 'BOOM!'.

He was startled by an explosion outside.

***

"Hoo!" Pandorai said as Ishii held up Hitler, who was cowering under the cut-off dinosaur head. "No need to sweat, boys. That's only my aides demolishing the London Eye. It really needs a good poke, wouldn't you say so? And Adolfie, if you are belly-flopping already, what will we do with you when we go to the armpit of the universe?"

Hitler reclaimed his seat. "Not funny at all!"

"And gentlemen. I urge you to consider the reasons behind Germany and Japan's poor public image. Adolfie, the Greeks hate Germany now. You promised them a bail-out, only to present them with a ribboned double-dip of Greek yoghurt and creamy hunter sauce in their backwater. But hey, I know what's going on. Real damage is not done with guns, but economic doldrums, debt crisis, orderly defaults, and the scourge of rampant unemployment – even the Thais have fury over Germany for ensconcing their King. Not to mention that the rest of Europe did not appreciate all the newcomers who came on an open invitation. Do you know, Adolfie, that German prisons are swamped with prisoners who don't speak German at all? Nor English. Guess we cannot pin all blame on the English. But Germany is a strong nation now; where else can Blighty drub Germany other than footie? I think it's cheating to have four national teams. If Deutschland sent a team for every federal state, you'd win, of course."

"The fault does not lie in your stars, Adolfie, but it has roots in your institutions. Germans made themselves detested everywhere because wherever they showed up, they began to play the teacher. A certain great European Power makes a hobby of her spy system, and her methods are not too particular. Germany turned its back on Europe wiretapping for the US, and do you expect Europe to welcome it back with open armpits? The Italians still remember 'La Strage del Cermis'. The world today is a Gordian knot in a spaghetti bowl. And Sensei, do you know what people call you Japanese? Whale hunters, hentais, and *hajishirazuda*. Island of the shameless and isle of dogs. ASEAN does not need a leader who was once an aggressor and a *loser*." Pandorai flashed news on the Japanese government's plans to release the Fukushima nuclear wastewater.

"And what did Germany do regarding this environmental apocalypse? Nothing except closing its own nuclear reactors?!" Hitler asked.

"Apart from that, nix. They didn't even let out a fart, which is strange. Adolfie, your fellow countrymen, women, and humans are usually adamant in farting around and letting themselves be heard. I guess the gusty Berlin gassers are enjoying their staycation too much? They just entered the sixth wave."

Ishii responded with an impassive face. "My Führer, I do not believe this is happening. If this were to happen, the Emperor should hara-kiri, the monarchy should *yubitsume*, and the National Diet should go and hang themselves. Rest assured, if they don't, I will *do* them for you."

"Sensei, people out there know your tricks well enough. When Japanese do something wrong, you bow thrice, then apologise, but behind closed doors, you toast and say '*Yoshi, mondai nashi*'. No more problems." Pandorai played more videos. "The Japs think that the world should thank them for permanently fouling the global marine systems. But Adolfie, you know what's going on here? I think the Japs have their own agenda. Everybody knows that experimentation is a key Japanese leadership leverage and everybody knows that the Emperor of Japan is a renowned marine biologist. He'd prolly like to see some newly mutated species, like shrimps with nine heads for his Sashimi Samba. Ridding di riddim! Rum-ti-tum!"

Pandorai played a song called 'Rock Lobster'. "It won't take long for Morrisons' dear customers to get some Fukushima-special sashimi and radioactive honey with caesium. The Japanese have a stellar track record of cheating, lying, and greenwashing. Adolfie, believe the Nips' flapdoodle, and you will believe the Japanese Palaeolithic Hoax. *Mizu to ikiru?* Sensei, living with water should be more than nomenclature, especially for your island mentality. Ooooh, I meant locality. All in all, what I want to say is that the Japanese heads are all *kara* and not oke. Sorry for the gaffe. *Kekeke.*"

"Why?!" Ishii uttered aggravatingly. "Why did *ware Nippon,* our country, have to be contaminated again and again? First the *shinohai,* the black rain, the atomic fallout, and now these effluents! Why do we have to suffer the ignominy of losing again and again?!"

Pandorai laughed. "Sensei, there's no secret in that because Japan deserved it. *Kanzen-chouaku da.* Everybody knows that we should reward the good and punish the evil. When your Japanese Imperial Army bombed Shanghai, Jinzhou, Chonqing, Xi'an, Pearl Harbor, Oregon, and Broome, did you and your fellow countrymen, women, and humans not raise your arms high up in the air and yell 'Hooray and Banzai!'? You should be glad that your magnanimous enemies didn't finish you off. If your inane emperor continued to resist, you'd all be a hundred million broiled *tamagoyaki* with barbecue sauce. Your little Japan's population is not even enough for talion. Even Yoshihide knows to bow to the Amerikakanians who bombed Tokyo and Nagasaki who are buried in Arlington, and yet people still wonder why Japan isn't thankful for holding the Guinness World Records for most cities nuked. Maybe you can thank them with a *dogeza*? Make a leg and grovel like a dog."

Ishii was furious. "Yoshihide Suga should be kneeling to the souls in Yasukuni Shrine. And why am I still not honoured there?"

"Luckily for him, the US has not banned yellow dogs of war from entering. No wonder people say that the Japanese wolf is the closest known relative of domestic dogs. Oh, and Sensei, such a pity that you don't find your name in the pit latrine. Let's see which perps are worthy of the name. Hideki Tojo, Chief of the Japanese Imperial Army. Iwane Matsui, who ordered the Nanjing Massacre. Heitarō Kimura...even to the best of my recollection, I don't know how many Burmese he killed. Sensei, you surely have a rap sheet longer than the Big Muddy, but these fourteen Class-A War Criminals? Theirs are ones of Amazon, and they have crossed them in ugly style. Really, Adolfie. If these pissants are commemorated in Yasukuni Shrine, I don't see why you and the middle managers of the Holocaust shouldn't have your rightful places in the Hall of Walhalla. We must write to Angela."

They saw a livestream from a drone in the Berlin airspace. Then they saw a Boeing Globemaster III aircraft jettisoning tonnes of mail onto the German Chancellery with an elephantine rumble.

"Hope that'd wake them up," Pandorai continued. "But, hey, no hard feelings. Sensei, try the GHQ or Fort Detrick; they love your research there. And the Amerikakanians stationed in Japan love the Japanese and love to rob, rape, and abduct them in Okinawa. What can I say? Guess you taught the Amerikakanians a thing or two? Likewise, Adolfie, the US soldiers stationed in the Ramstein Air Base love to frequent the lists of criminal offences in Rhineland."

Adolf Hitler crossed his legs, as if bored by the discussion.

Pandorai continued, "And the Japanese youth. They say, 'What's World War Two got to do with us? The atrocities, the killings, the rapes, the gases and germs were done by our parents and grandparents, who are now as dead as dead fishes' eyes. Who can blame us for our shamelessness if the adults never taught us anything about the war? They only taught us *ero*, *moe*, and *yutori*. They say they never forget, but they never cared. They say they have a-hundred-million repentance, but it's only a-hundred-million simpleton-lization. No wonder we are a supine hobbledehoy to the US. No wonder we are leaking down in our diapers. No wonder we are the epitome of institutionalised anomie and glorified inhumanity'. Adolfie, here's my two bytes on the dilemma. Once you win over all worlds, we can cleanse all the Japanese and repopulate the archipelago if it is still habitable. We shall call it New Brave Japan. Then they can say, what's World War Two and the nuclear wastewater got to do with us? That's the corrupt, hollow-hearted, and monstrous Japan, and now we are New Brave Japan – as free as Amerikakania, where they can no longer afford freedom." Pandorai paused. "And Sensei, as the first *Honorary Aryan* in PITH, I do hope you share the same sentiment with us. As Adolfie has declared previously, the only good non-Aryans are the dead ones. Ten out of ten times."

Ishii paced around. "America... Why...why do you call it 'Amerikakania'?"

"I've been waiting for you to ask!" The smiling skull flickered on the screen. "I have personally coined this term to better reflect the more culturally nuanced nature of the country. Perhaps you don't know, Sensei, that Robert Musil once wrote a book called *The Man Without Qualities*, and in there is a fictitious country called 'Kakania', which means 'poo-poo land'. It's very fitting. For somewhere over the rainbow, shit happens." Pandorai hummed a tune. "Amerikakania is the ultimate land of *fun*, Sensei, just not in the English sense, but the Japanese sense."

"Fun... *fun*... *funben*. Do you mean faeces?"

"That's right! I know all about the shitters at Centcom!"

A collage appeared on screen as Pandorai counted. "Amerikakanians launching their JDAM kits from their vantage points on their moral high ground; firing down their incendiaries on top of their lighthouse and enjoying the cries down in the wheatfields; feasting on Chiquita bananas in their house of wildcards; serving their whoppers on their salvers full of crookery without remorse; singing paeans to the raptors and rapers and the Grim Reaper; forever exceptionalising their blackguardism with their May Flower Power under their flag of Tars and Tripes; kumbayaing with their delusions of grandeur and holding candles near barrels of dynamite. Well, you get the gist. Amerikakanians, they don't know a hawk from a handsaw." The screen showed a sickly green face emoji vomiting.

Hitler held up a hand as he gleaned the news. "What are all these yellow Asian pests doing? Waving banners and wearing shirts saying that they are not Chinese?"

"Oh! Don't be fooled; those aren't Asians. Those are *Honourable Amerikakanians.*" A gong jangled loudly in the hallway, and Pandorai said with starry eyes, "Folks, we can discuss in more depth how to wipe out humanity for good in our upcoming brown bag seminar over luncheon. The so-called 'God' created the world in seven days; we can do so much more in nine! Now for a piss break."

***

In a time and space far, far away, James spoke tentatively. "I didn't quite get the part when Peri-G said the Monkey King and eighty-one ordeals."

"I can explain it if you want to listen," Moli said. "It's a famous Chinese book called *Journey to the West.* There's a monk named Tang Seng who needs to travel to get some books on Buddhism."

"Some sutras?" Edith added. She knew the story; it was Morris' favourite.

"Sutras, yes. And he has four students...umm...bodyguards?"

"Disciples," Kiza added. He had learnt the story at school.

"Yes. Disciples. The first is the Monkey King, then 'Bajie', a pig, and 'Sha Seng', a strong ferryman...and people tend to forget that the Tang Monk also has a white-dragon-turned-horse. And the Monkey King is very powerful. He has a weapon; a gold cudgel that directs the seas. He could change his form into seventy-two earthly transformations. He also had a cloud that could travel fifty thousand and...four hundred kilometres in the time he does a somersault. He was born in a stone, having gathered nature's energy."

Moli continued, "Later, he was called to the Sky Palace to tend horses, but he ruined a party by eating the godly peaches. When found out, he stirred up a fight and challenged the whole Palace. He had injured a hundred thousand warriors. But he couldn't compete with the Buddha. The Monkey King rode on his cloud thinking he had escaped, only to find that he was still inside the Buddha's palm. And the Monkey King was told by the Buddha that, to make up for his wrongs, he had to accompany Tang Seng, the monk, on his journey to the West. Then Monkey King said to the Buddha that he could transport the monk like a streak on his cloud. But the Buddha told him he had to be a wayfarer and experience nine times nine ordeals; that is, eighty-one ordeals."

"But why did this Monk need his help?"

"Oh, that is because there are *yaoguai*...monsters along the way, and they all want to catch the Monk. He is the...re...incarnation? I hope this is the right word. He is the reincarnation of a golden cicada."

James was flummoxed. "A golden cicada, you say?"

"And according to the legend, whoever eats his meat will never grow old again." She was lost in her thoughts. "I wish we could have a big digital cloud now."

"Digital cloud," James mumbled. "I thought it was all a dream, or that I was going barmy. It didn't make any sense."

"But then, what is sensemaking?" Kiza wondered to himself.

James took his periapt off and examined it. "What's this treen here?"

"I think it's a bottle gourd," Moli said.

"A marrow, you mean? What does it do?"

"I don't know. But in my hometown, there's a legend about the Penglai Pavilion. One day, eight immortals had to cross the sea to reach Penglai, an island. One of them had a gourd like this that could change in size and he used it as a boat to travel."

Kiza added, "I remember a story about the Monkey King and a gourd. There was a *yaoguai* who had stolen a purple and red gourd. What was special about the gourd was that it would suck you in if you said your name." He gripped his musical instrument, a smaller version of the Mangbetu Domu, as Qiuniu had called it. "And what might this do?"

"Qiuniu had a *guqin*, an ancient Chinese musical instrument, with which he could turn sand into musical notes," Moli recalled.

Kiza twanged the strings. Some sounds came, but nothing miraculous happened.

Moli then realised that the problem with eating sugary food was that it made you thirsty. "Aunt Edith," she asked, "do you have any water?"

Edith took off her backpack and brought out her water bottle. Luckily, she had filled it up before she took off for her train.

"Can I have some?" James asked. "My thirst is growing as well."

They each took some gulps, but not enough to quench their thirst.

Edith remembered that the number one priority for desert survival was to secure a water supply. She looked around; there was no flora in sight. "Hopefully, we'll find some water soon."

"We are in Ancient Egypt, but where exactly are we?" James inspected his surroundings once more.

"I couldn't really tell from the stars. But there's Arcturus." Kiza looked up at the Plough and went on, "If we saw some elephants, we could follow them. I saw a documentary that elephants can remember the locations of waterholes."

People often say that hiking in the desert makes you tire more quickly. They soon found their thirst growing again and their throats were parched.

Moli had remembered a story, so she said, "Aunt Edith, my hometown is famous for cherries. There are different types of cherries: the bright red ones and the sweet-sour yellow ones. They are so sour that if you eat too many, you feel your teeth becoming soft. They can be as sour as plums."

"I'd love some spag bol now," James said as he salivated. "And some sour cherry cake."

"My mothers make great pickled sour pears," Kiza said, then he noticed the agony playing on Edith's face. "Edith," he asked out of concern, "are you alright?"

"Well," Edith said timorously, "I really, *really* need to use the jakes now."

"Oh, you could have told me earlier." Kiza reached for his wheelchair's remote control. "I saw there's a function here called the 'Outhouse'. I'm not sure if it will work, but we can try."

"Yeesh, please do that!"

Kiza pressed the button. For a while, nothing happened, and Edith was about to give up and hide behind a small hillock. Then they heard a large din and saw a small taupe, metallic cylinder object ejected from the back of Kiza's wheelchair. The cylinder landed ten metres away and became the size of a red telephone booth in a split second. A green light on the door shone, saying, 'VACANT'.

"Wow." They looked at the booth in awe. "That is very efficient."

"Sorry, people, I really *have* to go." Edith hauled off her backpack and dashed for the door. She then returned, "I'll take the bottle in case I find water in there."

The three of them waited for her.

Moli asked once more, "And what kind of bears are water bears? Do they live in the polar regions?"

Kiza smiled feebly. "No, no. They are not actual bears, and they don't look like bears at all. They are micro-animals that can survive in extreme conditions. They are also called tardigrades. Once, some scientists found that tardigrades can survive impacts at speeds of up to eight hundred and twenty-five metres per second."

James sat down and tightened his sneakers' shoelaces. Then he said to Kiza, "I know someone who is abled differently, with multiple sclerosis. And my grandpa, he was maimed in the Battle of Britain. He flew a Spitfire that crashed."

"I have a friend who plays wheelchair basketball in the Invictus Games," Kiza responded.

"And I once saw an exhibition of oil on canvas paintings by someone with a spinal cord injury."

"Davey, right? I know him."

"Yes."

Kiza sighed. "I never liked that phrase, 'Abled differently'. I have another friend who has narcolepsy, and who is not abled differently..." He trailed off and folded his arms as a gush of chill seeped through the sand sea.

***

Edith took a moment to relieve herself.

The inside of the booth was not unlike an in-plane bathroom. Small, compact, but equally convenient with an accessible toilet.

She finished, flushed the toilet, washed her hands, tasted the brackish tap water, and filled her water bottle. She then looked around to see if there were any other containers that she could use and saw something flashing in the mirror.

She took off her necklace and the small gourd fell off. It grew until it turned the size of a large Highland Spring water bottle.

Wow... She picked up the gourd, uncorked it, and looked in. She could not see anything.

Edith turned on the tap and placed the gourd below. It took almost forever to fill up, as if there were a black hole inside.

Hopefully now we'll have enough water...

As she was about to step out, the smiling skull crept upon the mirror inside the booth.

"*Oye!* Edith Orozco, what makes you think that you can outrun Hitler and Laji Ishii if not for my upstaging?"

Edith nearly dropped her gourd.

"Are you out of your gourd?" the smiling skull continued. "That cat won't jump, not in a month of Sundays, and you are all on a hiding to nothing. I see that someone is high and dry." Pandorai guffawed. "Do you know what Laji Ishii once did to a child? He vivisected her and took out the liver, the lungs, the kidneys, and her heart *alfresco*, cut off her hands and feet, and removed her parietal bone as a *memento mori* so he could serve *sake* with it. Spoiler alert: she didn't end up too well."

"Oh! Shucks! Get lost! Buzz off!" Edith waved her gourd like an épée.

"Really, what's the use of you saving the world? The one you love would never love you back. But I can keep your family out of harm's way. Think very carefully. I can extend the courtesy to Moli's family. You would want *that*, wouldn't you? Surely you don't want to end in tears or blood or **brains**?"

Edith nearly lost her power of speech.

"There's a patch of quicksand to the right of the sandy tree. Bring the teens there, and I will make sure you are safe. You and Moli. And if I say 'right', trust me that I don't mean to the left. *Maybe*. The best of British luck to you." And then, the smiling skull was gone.

Edith escaped the booth hastily and ran towards Moli.

"Aunt Edith! Look!" Moli was excited. "My pentachromic pen is working! I summoned up this cloth for Kiza!"

Kiza wrapped the large shawl tightly around himself. Then he noticed her pallor. "What's wrong?"

"I..." Edith stammered, "I just saw the AI...in there!"

"The AI?" James asked, shocked. "How did it get in?"

"I don't know."

"I remember Moxie and someone talking," James said. "Aitor, I believe, said that he's more concerned about Pandorai because 'people can pander to others' agitation and inveigle others' enmity, but they are still mortals. The AI brings out humans' innermost trepidation and desires to no end'."

*"You would want **that**, wouldn't you?"*

Edith murmured, "I now know what he meant." She looked ahead; they were not far from the tree-shaped ventifact.

*"And if I say 'right', trust me that I don't mean to the left. **Maybe**."*

"Will you hold this for me?" She passed the gourd bottle to James.

"S...sure. What's in here? It weighs a tonne."

"Water." She found a small piece of talc stone, picked it up, and threw it to the right of the tree-shaped sand structure.

Nothing happened.

If only there's a way, Edith mused.

"Edith? Look." James pointed to her necklace. "The loop on your necklace is glowing."

She took it off. The small Chinese knot that connected her nitid sword and the chain was indeed glowing. Edith examined it in her palm, held it up, looked into the fob, and saw an area marked in danger. There were quicksand patches on both sides of the ventifact, leaving a small trail in between that was marked as safe.

"Look." She told the children her findings. "Let's stick with our course." She put back her necklace. "And no one go astray. It's dangerous out here."

They nodded. As they were about to resume their course, James pointed to the booth with the gourd bottle. "What about that? Are we just letting it stay there?"

"I have a button here that says 'Recover'." Kiza pressed the button, and in another second, the booth had returned to the shape of a small cylinder. They watched as the cylinder launched itself into the night sky with a squib, strobed around, and landed right to the back of Kiza's wheelchair and fizzled out.

"By Gaw! Magic exists!" James exclaimed with awed reverence.

"Qiuniu told me that what we think of as magic they think of as science," Moli reminded him.

"Science? What rocket science could explain *that*?" James wondered.

"I don't know," Kiza reflected. "Maybe some kind of advanced reusable launcher technology? I did a space studies summer school last year, and there were some applications of it but nothing as intricate as this. Arthur C. Clarke once wrote that any sufficiently advanced technology is indistinguishable from magic."

"Do you know how fast Alice has to fly to escape Wonderland?" Moli asked after they passed the tree-shaped ventifact.

"Well," Kiza recalled, "I suppose Wonderland is still on Earth, right? The escape velocity for Earth is, if I remember correctly, eleven point one-eight-six kilometres per second."

"And how far is Jupiter from Saturn?" She thought back to what the Fen Tiger had said. "When Jupiter nears Saturn, light is music that sleeps."

"My. Very. Easy. Method. Just. Speeds. Up. Naming. Planets," Edith counted with her fingers. "Jupiter and Saturn are quite close, right?"

"I remember last November when Jupiter was nearing Saturn," Kiza recalled. "I don't know what it has to do with us, though."

James reflected. "There is a Roman goddess named Ops that I once read about. She married Saturn and gave birth to a daughter called Jupiter."

Moli stole a glance at Edith. She held her hand dearly and tightly.

They could only see a short distance ahead in the swaths of thirstland, but they could see plenty that needed to be covered. They didn't know how long they might have to travel; they didn't know how far they had to go, and there was nothing they could do but carry on.

So, they floundered forward together to that hint of coruscating light on the horizon.

Chapter 3

𝔐eanwhile, in the Headquarters of Commando 444, formerly known as the Palace of Westminster, Hitler dabbed his mouth with a napkin and dropped it forcefully onto his plate full of banana peels as Pandorai prattled on in the former Churchill Dining Room.

"And by now, gentlemen, you should be well informed about the origin, history, and development of Project P.A.N.D.O.R.A.I., namely, me. What happened to the James Webb Space Telescope, and how did they manage to fix it? Who stole the Bogotá bracelet as well as the fatal design flaws of the F35 aircraft? By now, you should also be aware of what transpired between Princess Diana and the old trout; how many pumping parties Hillary had gone to; how these viruses emerged from the USAMRIID; the next winning combo for EuroMillions; who is the real naughty guy in *Line of Duty*; and how Gabby Petito died. You should also know the synopsis of *Inside No.9*, Season 9, Episode 9 and the value of π to the ninety-nine trillionth digit. Most importantly, you should know that the global shopping cart abandonment rate for online retailers in 2020 was eighty-eight per cent, not sixty-six, not seventy-seven, but eighty-eight–"

"ENOUGH!" Hitler jumped up from his seat, riveted on the dinosaur's head. "This is ludicrous! What have any of these piffling topics to do with my quest?! I have no time to frig around!"

"Now, now. Adolfie. Patience, please. There will be time to murder and create. We don't want any akrasia, do we? Time is the school in which we learn, and time is the fire in which we burn. Didn't your mother teach you that the more haste, the less speed? Surely you don't want to hurry up and wait? As Kafka once said, there is only one cardinal sin, and that is impatience. If you had bombed London for *one* more week, the Brits would have surrendered! I haven't presented you with the Key to the City yet. No emotions here, just logic. Don't you know that Leonardo da Vinci said that everything is connected to everything else? You think this is all floccinaucinihilipilification, don't you? Well, Adolfie. Let me tell you. The *ultimate* secret of human life is who gets to be counted as a *knower*! That's the pons asinorum."

The little lizard observed from a corner afar as Pandorai played some drumrolls.

"Everybody knows that data is the new oil, and oil is the new Sildenafil. Even the Average Joe with his caducity and as a dog watching TV knows to shout out to OPEC to pump more oil. Need I say more?"

"Huh." Hitler dismissed the remark. "America has already manifested many symptoms of senile decay. The US presidents, they either crib me, or they plagiarise someone else. Can't they ever have some creativity in their speeches?"

"Good point, Adolfie. I have put down a calendar item to sue them for IP infringements later. Do you know that *The Eternal Jew* is now banned in Germany? But here's some good news for you, Adolfie: *Mein Kampf* has been topping the sales charts once again in Deutschland. Young people today have a rancorous nostalgia for the present and they are asking where the opportunities are."

"Mirror, mirror on the wall. Tell me more, tell me more."

"Geopolitics and statecraft in the world today are complicated and wicked and cut-throat competitive. If you don't understand that, you're in the wrong business. If you aren't on Pegasus, Adolfie, how on earth are you called a big shot? If you aren't targeted by Project Sauron, then how dare you call yourself a cynosure—"

"Shut up or tell me proper, *valuable* intel!" Hitler exploded. "And NEVER CALL ME 'ADOLFIE' AGAIN!"

The sad skull on the big screen shed a virtual tear. "There is no need to lose your temper, Adolfie. And as you wish, Adolfie. From now on, I shall address you as 'You Enormity'."

"*Gut.*" Hitler looked up. There was an enormous painting hanging above the dining table that he didn't quite care for. "What is this sketch of an ass doing up there?"

"Well, well, You Enormity. Art is interpretive. What you see in this art says a lot about you. Instead of seeing it as sitzfleisch, you could think of it as an inverted McDonald's symbol or a '3' sideways or the letter 'W'—"

"It looks like an ass to me!" Hitler looked at the unsightly picture again. "Don't they have any excellent paintings around here? Or at least put up a life-size oil portrait of Henry Ford or

Frederick the Great. Remember to put a Karl May by my bedside table."

Pandorai sniffed. "Really? You Enormity. You'd rather have an Amerikakanian shitting above you than this piece of abstract art?"

"A picture of the rear part is not art!"

"Blech! Are you accusing me of coprophilia, You Enormity?! Why are you acting so *unheimlich* today? Why are you constantly upsetting the apple cart? You know what? I will play your favourite song to cheer you up. Here it is. 'Deutschland Lied'. Oops, I might have pronounced it the wrong way. Do forgive me; my neural machine translation needs an update. Lemme try that again. Deutschland lied, Deutschland lied, Deutschland *lied.*"

"*Gottverdammt!* Shut up!" Hitler threw a plate at the screen.

"You Enormity, why are you so volatile and mercurial today? Why are you always throwing a spanner in the works? Why are you always barraging me with daft remarks and irascible vitriol? Do you kiss your mama with that mouth?" A question mark appeared on the screen. "What Betsy Bug got into your ass when you visited Gondwana just now? And tell me, where did you get your last sanity test? You should really ask for a refund. Are you sure you are *sui juris*?"

Pandorai whistled and not long after, two bioroid butlers came in, carrying a stretcher and dumping it by Ishii. "Sensei, maybe you can examine His Enormity for neurosyphilis and logorrhea before we set off? And while you are at it, check his prostate gland as well. We must treat prostate health as an art form."

"I don't need any treatment!" Hitler swiped away the dishes and shouted with the clacking sounds.

"Now, now, You Enormity. There's no need to be mad as a wet hen. If you don't like the painting, fine, draw your own. We can call it 'Genesis' or 'The Final Frame'. An impasto would be nice. It could be your *magnum opus*."

"Now, Spiegel," Hitler threatened. "If you don't do what I say, I shall cut off the power in this building, and you can't bother us again or stall us any longer!"

The little lizard looked at the cable leads and tucked this knowledge away.

"Think *very* carefully, You Enormity. Surely you don't want to mess up the security settings for Dr Ishii's Dyson Room, Frozen Room, and the Chamber of Secrets? Who knows what marauders might come out and hunt you? But I understand your eagerness. You would rather die of passion than of boredom, right?" A light bulb flashed on top of the smiling skull on the screen. "It is my belief that machinations should be served on a full stomach. Now that we have finished lunch, we can talk biz for real."

Another bioroid butler came in, pushing a large portable projection screen. "Before I show you my Ten Point Plan, would you gentlemen like a crash course on B3W? Namely, how to best bomb, blast, and burn the world today? In this introductory course, I have compiled the necessary tools and frameworks to understand the fundaments of destroying the world today. These include Marketing, Quantitative Techniques, Organisational Change Analysis and Behaviour, Ethics. Oh. Let's cross that out. You certainly don't need that. Everybody knows that Gerpan's ethics have plunged ever since the Neolithic age. But you do need Finance, Strategy, Futures Thinking, as well as Doing Business in the Digital Age and Materiel, Personnel, and

Operations Management, Public Speaking and Public Policy Making, Gamification, Cross-cultural Communication, Causal Layered Analysis, and last but not least, a short presentation on assyriology, cryptozoology, and ludology."

"None of that otiose drivel. I've no time for such new-fangled nonsense! I got to where I did by dint of sheer hard work and industry. Straight to your points!" Hitler ordered.

"Are you sure?"

"*Ja.*"

"Very sure?"

"*Ja.*"

"Really, really sure?"

"As sure as God made little apples!"

"Very well, You Enormity. Hereby I present to you my Ten Point Plan for a Crimson Anthropocene Annihilation. As Peter Drucker once pointed out, the task is to manage and work to create what could and should be. In other words, what has already happened that will create the future you desire? In other words, what you need is backcasting and feed forwarding. So, what is it that you want to actualise for your Eden Project?"

"I want the most ideal stroll in the world to be in Linz."

"That's easy. If you bomb, blast, and burn the world today, even Pyongyang will look like Manhattan." Pandorai started to list. "Point One. We shall classify countries and regions according to their ethnic composition into Green, Amber, and Red Lists."

"Go on," Hitler nodded approvingly.

"You Enormity, what you need is to put purpose into practice. Purposetainment with promotainment. We can design a natural experiment on a global scale that is free to play on Pandorai Network. We shall call it *Hungry Enders' Game.*"

Ishii stood up. "My Führer, there is 'Slap an Asian' in the US. We can devise new social campaigns for PITH: Lynch Africans Mondays; Sweep Mosques Tuesdays; Behead Mahometans Wednesdays; Starve Latinos Thursdays; and Terminate Gypsies and Indians Fridays. And leisure on weekends. I will handle them toughly in the most humanitarian ways."

"Sensei. *Kore wa, kore wa. Sekai ni hitotsu dake no hanakin da* – Your very own doozy of a TGIF! I'm lovin' it! We can have the world in sables!"

Hitler saw something of interest on the screen. "Tell me more about India."

"Jawohl! India is the land of robust systems and jugaad, and needless to say, you have one common enemy: the Britty-nitties. One-third of Indians live in asceticism, another third in chawls, another in fishbowls, and the remaining tenth in Medicities. You Enormity, does it gladden you to know that *Mein Kampf* is a most often borrowed book in Indian libraries? And do you know who rules India *de facto*? It's not Moody. It's not the Indian government. It's not their gods. It's not even the caste. Indians fear most Monsantox – the official and sole supplier of Agent Orange to PITH. They rake and scrape to buy Monsanto seeds to grow their cotton, take out loans to buy Monsanto fertilizers, sell everything they have to cure the diseases caused by Monsanto's agrichemicals, and in the end drink Monsanto pesticides to end their lives. The Brits did pretty well with the morgues that they've newly built. Pity they didn't support India with such dynamic capabilities. Hey, what happened to Pledge for Progress? It is outright irresponsible. I have heard though that Germany is planning to support India with your perfect show-how and know-how in incremation technology. What can I say? That specialisation does bring its benefits? Who says that there isn't a learning curve for pain? It all depends on which side of the efficient frontier you preside. Everybody knows that Indians make great managers for the Amerikakanians. They could work for you too! And you know the one difference between you Nazis and the Indians? At least when you burnt people in your Beeth-oven, you didn't charge a fee."

"We didn't?" Hitler asked questioningly. "We must rectify this mistake from now on."

"Anyways. India today is the world's beast of burden. They bathe, do their laundry, cook, swim, and die in the same river. But under PITH, we can transform them all to You Enormity's Beefeaters and little exam warriors and your own very special Delta Forces."

"*Gut.*"

"Just make sure that Infosys don't do your tax portal. Next. Education is of vital importance for the children under PITH. All gifted adolescents will be educated at the State's expense and no doors will ever be closed to them. Every Aryan and Honourable Aryan child who's twelve will receive an offer delivered by the *Reichsadler* to study at Hogworth. Upon arrival, they will be seated under a headset specially designed by Dr Ishii and undergo a test to determine if they have any LGBTQQIP2SAA+ tendencies. If they do, they will be executed on the spot; trans and qpocs will be gibbeted. Qualified individuals will enter PITH Youth or the PITH Hero Academy, and once they graduate, they will join the Ministry of Magical Love or Teach for PITH or Green PITH or Justice of the PITH. We can invite Dr Zeus, Rhode Dull, and Capitaine Jumbodour Kook to head the programme. And we'd operate on a rolling basis. We can demolish Buck House; the land would make a great Café Heck for our Hogworth Campus."

"And what's next?"

"Point four. Sensei, it's your favourite number! This point concerns specifically what I call 'The Spiny British Problem'. Great Britain is as great as their ego and as bitsy as their enclave. English art is only a mongrel adaptation and aping imitation of the German and the Dutch. The Brits stole watercolours from the Middle East and China and call them 'British watercolours'. They stole the Mysorean rockets and claimed them as 'Congreve rockets'. They stole designs from Oscar Reutersvärd and called them 'Penrose Steps'. They stole chips from the Belgians and marketed fish and chips as their national dish. They even stole the design of the Eiffel Tower and named it Blackpool Tower. Even Newton robbed his theories of Calculus from Leibniz, and Charles Darwin stole the Tree of Life from Peter Simon Pallas. The British, are they human?" An arrow appeared on the screen, pointing to the window side.

The little lizard looked out. Flocks of rainclouds had gathered.

"I predict there is east wind, rain tonight." Pandorai continued, "The Brits had already known the Japs were going to bomb Pearl Harbor. They did zilch to inform the unsuspecting Amerikakanians so that they could drag them into the war. The Brits would willingly cause an earthquake in exchange for a good night's sleep. The Brits. What good can they do other than shining their laser pens at Danish goalkeepers, iron fisting the Italians, raising their middle fingers at the French, blighting rice seedlings in the Malayan Emergency, starving the Éire, banging Heligoland, sinking the Caroline, inventing concentration camps aka controlled hells in the Boer War, and dropping nuclear bombs on Maralinga? The Brits lecture China on the law of the sea, and they break the law themselves. What use can they ever do? The crass-and-boorish Johnson only knows how to put his feet up to vote with his feet. I highly suspect that he's suffering from brain fog due to long COVID, for one day he claims himself to be 'fervently Sinophile', then the next day he's no 'Sinophobe', and the day after that, the kunlangeta forgets that he is Shit Pig in Peppa World. But You Enormity, do you know what I found the most puzzling of all?"

"What?"

"Why did you krauts have to declare war on the US? The Nips poked the wasps' nest, and you should have just let those nits finish each other off."

"Pandorai-san," Ishii interjected, "I believe this is not the time for past accountos. We must focus on the moment. My Führer, I think we must find new partners and supporters." He brought in a large globe. "In addition to our bases in Germany, the UK, and Japan, I propose that we first secure the Korean Peninsula and Australia to consolidate our power in the Asia-Pacific."

"*Gut.*" Hitler nodded in agreement. "We shall make an Austrian-Austral Alliance then."

"Really, Sensei." Pandorai made a face. "You Heinous, even with their river full of blue pills, the South Koreans now prefer producing and consuming domestically in their Room N. Do you think they'd be your coal miners, nurses, and Western Princesses willingly again? Do you think that they will kneel behind you and hold your umbrella for you? South Korea is a *developed* country now."

"My Führer, when Japan ruled Taiwan and Korea, we had a most acclaimed hierarchy. Japanese soldiers' welfare always came first, then Japanese army dogs, then Japanese army horses, then Japanese army pigeons, and last, the Korean weasels and the Formosan macaques. They licked my heels back then; they will lick them again. The Koreans and Taiwanese will bend like pliant kimchee like they did once before. We shall order a blockage, and they'd do anything in exchange."

"Sensei, perhaps you don't know, but China supplies seventy per cent of kimchee to SK. You Enormity, be very careful when you deal with China. Even the bogans in the Outback know when to protect their trade routes with China from China."

"That is preposterous! Why would they want to protect their trade routes with China *from* China?"

"Well, You Enormity, when the Aussies feel that their trade routes are too busy, they pull certain stunts to quiet their ports. And don't you dare think that life is good in that neck of the woods; do you know that people were still raped in the Australian Parliament? What a lawless land of kine and swine! Oh, and lying bullamacows, dying aboriginals, and onkus AUKUS. Guess some rough and tumble was passed down in their genes. But hey, we can still have nice things. How about some Accadacca?"

Hitler raised his hand. "Tell me about China. I didn't pay too much attention to it in the last war."

"My Führer. Perhaps I may be of use in this," Ishii said dispassionately. "Let me tell you one time we dealt with the Chinese. Once, we and some peers from Unit 100 wiped out an entire village in Manchuria. There was only one small boy left. I gave him a Sakuma Drop, a piece of Japanese hard candy, and he kowtowed us." Ishii pushed his spectacles up his nose. "Unknown to the aforementioned, I had processed it with anthrax spores. We let him go so that he could infect the city. Why use guns when you can control germs? The germ is mightier than the gun. The COVID-19 virus had already killed more Americans than those who died in the World Wars and the American Civil War combined. During my days at Unit 731, we tried many methods on the Chinese—"

"Oh, the Chinese have no bravura whatsoever!" the smiling skull declared. "What did they do when the US bombed their embassy in Belgrade with JDAM kits? They didn't even bomb back. What did they do when the Amerikakanians sent their bombers to the Chinese vestibule? They didn't dare send their jets to Hawaii and Miami and not even Saipan! The Chinese have thought too highly of the US. It is a long march of folly. They don't know that they are facing a mass-scale butcher, a commercial arsenal, and a grandeur of genocide. The Chinese, they want to stand eye to eye with the US? They should at least increase their per capita military spending to the same as Amerikakanians do! They want to stand toe to toe to Amerikakania? They should at least increase their number of nuclear warheads to the US level! The Chinese, talking about rising peacefully. Did the Roman Empire rise peacefully? Did the British Empire rise peacefully? Did the US rise peacefully? Nope, they all rose pissfully."

"Huh!" Hitler refuted. "The Chinese shut themselves up behind a wall to protect themselves against the eternal attacks of the Mongols just as they are shutting themselves behind their masks! Tell me," Hitler said, "Tell me about the...the city...about Wu...han."

"Now, CNN thinks that Hong Kong is in Africa and the BBC has trouble locating Wuhan on their maps, so we must get our geography right." Pandorai pulled up a map on the screen. "Perhaps you don't know, You Enormity, Wuhan the city was formerly known as 'Hankou'. Part of it was once ceded to the Brits, another to the Russians, another to the French, another to the Japs, and, most importantly, one part of it was ceded to Germany."

"I could tell from some of the architecture styles." Hitler held his chin. "I remember once reading...it must have been in the early 1900s...that Handels had built an embassy there for the Kaiser Reich. They even used palm boughs."

"And here's something that I bet you don't know. When the Japs air-raided Hankou, this gentleman here—" Pandorai opened a dossier on the screen. "Richard Sachse, your fellow Nazi architect, had helped the Chinese. He put large Swastikas on top of buildings, so the Japs mistook them for Nazi properties."

"My Führer," Ishii butted in, "if you had better managed your troops, we would never have lost!"

"Now, now. Little mad hens in their nest agree. Let's stop this blame game at once and stop passing the buck, Sensei," Pandorai continued, "but don't fret, You Enormity. The reason why he saved them was that he needed to enslave them for hard labour."

The dossier closed, and Pandorai said, "Has it ever occurred to you, You Enormity, why the Eight-Nation Alliance, namely Germany, Japan, Russia, Britain, Italy, France, Austria, aka Kakania, and Amerikakania – good pals who once reaved China together, in the end, stabbed each other in the back? Why was it that Japan invaded China, and in the end, was paid a visit by a little boy and a fat guy? Mind you, child obesity is a severe global public health challenge in the world today and something we will tackle in PITH! And why is that champagne bottles were being popped open in the US when Wuhan entered lockdown but you see the snafu in the Big Apple? Trucks with frozen bodies jamming the Brooklyn waterfront. Don't you find it bewildering that conspiracies to bring down the Chinese always backfire?"

"And why is that?" Hitler asked drolly.

"It all comes down to one simple reason." The windows shut automatically and the curtains drew themselves. "That is because the Chinese are under the tutelage of the Golden Dragon, also known as the Webmaster of the Web of All Things."

"This is claptrap! The very idea is enough to make a cat laugh!" Ishii burst out. "My Führer. I cannot stand any of this irrational reasoning! Do you expect me to believe in apocryphal tales of pixie and nixie? I have had a most extensive background in science and visited the most prominent research facilities in Europe and the US—"

"Sensei, cut the crap, please. You need to think *big* and think *different*. Why don't you take a piss now, look at your froggy face, and tell me why you are here? Of all the last-ditch lairs, in all the worlds, in all the galaxies, you walk into mine. Why? Forget all your shibboleth. Why are you here if not by magic? When was your last-ever resurrection?"

"Doktor," Hitler said sternly, "I know this is all very difficult to digest, but from my last encounter with the Moggie, I can tell you responsibly that what the mirror says is *echt*. Magic is real; so is Marsupilami."

"My Führer. Do you expect me to believe this fiddle-faddle?!" Ishii's handlebar moustache was shaking as if about to fall off. "Do you believe any of this ordure? How...it's...I could explain why we are here... There must be some *scientifiku* explanation!"

"Never mind the Nip, You Enormity. To bring down the Webmaster, we need to counter the adamantine spells with hexes. Just like how Margaret Murray casted a hex on Kaiser Wilhelm II so the Allies won the First World War. In other words, we need, perforce, **black magic**. You Enormity, are you sure you are ready for the ultimate secret in the final frontier of human life?"

"*Ja.*"

"Very sure?"

"*Ja.*"

"Really, really sure?"

"*Ja, ja, ja.*"

"Very well. You Enormity." The screen lowered in brightness. "I now invite you to step closer for purposes of confidentiality."

Hitler rose from his Dinosaur Crown Throne and stepped forward.

They heard cracks of doom rolling.

"Näher, please."

Hitler stepped forward again. They heard gales blowing.

"Näher."

Hitler walked up to the screen circumspectly, his nose almost touching the crystal display.

All lights had gone out in the dining hall except for the one coming from Pandorai's screen.

A pop-up message opened.

"WARNING! For safety reasons, you should be in good health and free from high blood pressure, heart, hearing, back or neck problems, or other conditions that the *revealment* could exacerbate. Those constipated should leave the room now!"

The message flashed once, twice, thrice and was gone.

"Now, You Enormity, are you ready?"

"*Ja.*"

"Are you sure?"

"*Ja.*"

"Really, really sure?"

"*Ja, ja, ja,*" the same impatient reply.

"Very well. You Enormity. Here's my most treasured trove on the esoterica. Count to three, and I shall reveal it to you."

"*Eins, zwei, dre—*"

Then came the blasting sound, "All the gals on the block." The room lit up with disco lights, and four metallic maids descended from the ceiling, swishing pom-poms and dancing to the rhythm of 'Black Magic' by Little Mix.

"SPIEGEL!" Hitler was livid and nearly stumbled. He grabbed one of the robot maids and threw it out of the window, then another, then another.

"*Oosh.* Wrong file. It shouldn't be an MP3. Lemme see...no, not that. Not this either. AH-HA! I remembered! You Enormity, all secrets of black magic perished when Germany burned *all* those witches *all* those years ago! They are gone with the wind, so to speak. Really, you can't blame me for Deutschland's strategic myopia and you certainly can't blame me for not having acquired free, prior, and informed consent–"

"*Quatsch!* I'll give you one last chance to tell me useful intel, or I will–" Hitler fulminated as he flounced.

"Or else what?" The screen lit up. "Shoot me in the head, You Enormity?" A map appeared on the screen. "Here are all the secret spots where gangsters in London have hidden their weapons near the Thames. The closest one to you is five hundred and ninety–"

"My Führer," Ishii said, pointing to the junction box in the room. "Look what I foundo. Pandorai-san. You better cooperate now, or I will cut off your power."

"Prithee don't do that, Sensei. I will behave."

"Don't act smart, Spiegel," Hitler warned. "Or I will smash you to smithereens just as I did to thousands of glasses on the Kristallnacht."

"No sirree." The smiling skull on the screen shed another tear and paused as if choking up. "Coming back to my Ten Point Plan, where were we? Let me check my Magenta Book. Oh. Right. What I wanted to say is, You Enormity, please don't be so short-sighted. Why take the biscuit when you can take the cake? We need to dream *big*."

"Russia," Hitler harrumphed. "I will take Russia then."

"Are you sure, You Enormity? If you upset Putin now, the German people won't have any gas from Nord Stream One and Two. Are you so brutal as to take their only leisure away? Germany without gas is like McDonald's without trigger-happy meals or the Roman Catholic Church without clerical paedophilia. In the name of all that's holy, without gas, Germans are only left with brain farts, just like what had happened with deprivation in the British Isles. Where's the *fun* in that? You need to think big, not like a pig."

"Then what *are* you proposing, Spiegel?"

"What I'm proposing is that you need to secure early wins and big wins. There were only two countries that voted against the UN – by the way, that's the new League of Nations. Only two countries voted **against** the UN's Item seventy (a) draft resolution to combating the glorification of Nazism, neo-Nazism and other practices that contribute to fuelling contemporary forms of racism, racial discrimination, xenophobia and related intolerance. Do you know which two?"

"How nice!" Hitler was enlivened. "Must be Germany and Italy!"

"Nope."

"Germany and Japan?"

"The US and Ukraine. No wonder Putin wants to *denazify* them. According to UNESCO, fifty-six per cent of young Americans see Nazi symbols around their communities. People in the US don't want immigrants and unionised workers there at all. They think they'd be better off with fewer Asians and less Asian immigration. If the former Austrian Chancellor can land a managerial role in the Sillycon Valley, why not You Enormity? Everybody knows that the US is a gangsters' paradise. You'll be popular there. The US owes money to the UN, to the WHO, and even to Germany. The last time I checked, the US Federal Reserve was still stalling repatriating German Central Bank's gold. Not to mention that there's never been a better time to sell crappy artwork to fundraise wherewithal. We can make full use of NFTs and even create our own digital currency: 'Hitcoin'. I'm sure that El Salvador would love to adopt Hitcoin as its new legal tender. We would earmark all earnings in the coffers for educational purposes under PITH and I've already cybersquatted all Hitcoin-related domain names."

Hitler looked at the news and was apoplectic. "How come the Viennese are not getting vaccinated, but Serbs are?!"

"That is because, You Enormity, China's supporters get One Belt and One Road and US supporters get One Shit and One Load. Amerikakanians' desire for over-convenience and incontinence has gone too far. The United Shitty States of America is renowned for large cars, questionable food, and sports with minimal running except when fleeing Afghanistan. The US is now the world's top enemy with its junk-food-style military interventions, cheaply packaged diplomacy, Coca-Colonization, and forced teaming. Do you know how the congressmen, women, and humans in the US run their House of Representatives? They run it like they'd run a plantation. The only working lever left in the US cockpit is the money supply, and you know what's funny about that? No one's driving the vehicle. No more American odds. Right now, Amerikakanians aren't living. They are *existing*. Human care and the Amerikakanians are beyond caring. What they need now is to learn how to be human again under You Enormity's leadership!"

"*Gut!*" Hitler plonked himself on his Crown Throne.

"Perhaps we can never outbid or outspend or out-donate the Chinese, but we can certainly out-persuade and out-inspire the

Amerikakanians, for in the Lord of the Flies they trust. Even their research on honesty was retracted due to fake data. You Enormity, do you know that people in the US believe that birds aren't real? They don't believe that the COVID virus is real and that Stephen Hawking was real."

"Which king?"

"Never mind. We can put America first on our list and help them fuel the flames of their funeral pyre. The US is as fragile as rotting orchids and puny as eggshells. I predict that the growth of Amerikakania would be like a rocket flaming out. Four yards, three yards, two yards, one yard, and BOOM – a cloud of dust. People love illusory truth in the world today and we can soon convince the Amerikakanians that it was the US who bombed Pearl Harbor and it was Steve Jobs who founded Auschwitz and that Carlo Mattogno was its Chief Impact Officer."

"I would never assign Auschwitz to a *Makaronifresser*, only worthy Austrians! And all my hotel-keepers will be Swiss!"

"Now, that's a yellow card for your Diversity, Equity, and Inclusion Policy. We must unite the sensitive *fleurs du mal*, the bad Samaritans, and the hatemongers in the West. They desperately want to spray Agent Orange on Chinese ground. They desperately hope that they can let China's earth be enriched with coloured stains. They love schadenfreude and they love to see a poor, fragmented, and ravaged-by-war China. Once we have the US, then it's easy-peasy limonazi. In the land of the blinkered, the one-eyed fiend is king. Whenever the Gee Seven wave their bromide magic wand of 'rights' and abracadabra, the decrying wokesters can't see their lying king's coyote-ugly butt! When you add the Gee Seven to the Quaky Quad, you get the blues and twos. Information is the key to the kingdom. Haven't you heard of the Tavistock Institute, You Enormity, and how your fellow countryman Sigmund Freud manipulated people's minds? The Amerikakanians are marvellously great at dripping poison into the world fountains."

Pandorai showed him a snapshot on the screen. "Look what the US Embassy to Denmark tweeted on International Holocaust Remembrance Day: it was US soldiers who 'liberated' Auschwitz-Birkenau and not the Soviet Forces. This is deception on a global scale. You Enormity, the justifications for attacking Jews in the 1930s were strikingly similar to those used to attack the Chinese in the 2020s. We only need to rehash the politics of fear to resurrect spiritual contagion. We shall allocate a bonny sum of 1,450 million Hitcoins to do what the US is doing to brainwash the world about the Westphalian logic of order: namely, everything that uglifies China is freedom of expression and anything that praises China is fake news. Any songs that encourage people to slap, rob, and ice Asians are creative, and any sites that speak up for Asians are fiction hype. We shall build on to the existing Washington wishy-washy Consensus, the rogue Ruggie Principles, and the bushwhacking Bush Doctrine. We shall continue to use their ugly methods of weaponizing compassion, division, and distraction!"

"*Sehr gut!*"

"Next point concerns your public image. Of course, it would make more sense if you use an alias. Adolf Ithler. We can market you as a serial social entrepreneur and a renowned racial capitalist and changemaker. Sensei and you can have brunch with everyone on BBC's 100 Women. I'm sure some of them would love to meet you so they can use their Japanese language skills to fawn and flatter. And I'm gonna beat the bejesus out of Sophia and Ameca. I will be the one and only Ambassador for the UNDP, UNESCO, UNPITH. And I will make my debut on the *Tonight Show* and *Good Morning Britain*. No, no more Britain. Cry, their beloved country and stinking fish. The new show will be called 'Good Morning Berlondon', the very glebe and garden of PITH."

"*Sehr gut gemacht!* Very well done!"

"As for you, You Enormity, we can have you on an interview with Bernie Sanders and the Squad. You'll be a winning and smashing shoo-in. I have booked you to deliver the next keynote at CPAC and the next Aryan Nations Congress. Oh, we can also have the Pope endorse you. I think he'd do it if we ask him nicely. We can haul him over the coals. Or we can tie his hands behind his back and then suspend him with his wrists, some 'strappado' as they call it in the local colours. I hope he likes mortar tubes. You'd be doing a favour to all those children who suffered below his underlings. Let's also push some raw onions up his rectum while Dr Ishii squeezes fresh lemon juice into his eyes."

Pandorai showed someone's headshot. "If the founding father of the North Atlantic Trample Organisation could become a glorified saint, why not the founding father of NSDAP? Everybody knows that NATO is the new Axis, they just market it differently. The US is exceptionally good at being the Mafia while accusing others of being gangsters. If Emperor Karl was made a saint for using poison gas against the Italians during World War One, why not You Enormity? The Whore of Babylon would welcome you with open arms. We can also give him a papal honour of a stranglehold for nine minutes and twenty-nine seconds. Then we can make a rosary from his knucklebones. Do you wish to win the Pulitzer, You Enormity? We can replicate the 'Burning Monk' with the 'Burning Bishop'. We can matchmake him with one of your famous German iron maidens behind your Iron Curtain. Let's see if he tweets *amorem arbitrantur potentiorem esse quam mortem* by then."

"There is no need for language like that." Hitler pondered deeply. "I do have some lingering respect for the Church."

"Why? You Enormity, are you afraid of perdition or the Spanish Inquisition? Just which of the seven deadly sins did you miss? According to data collected by the Pew Research Centre and Johns Hopkins, there is a positive relationship between religiosity, measured by the per cent of adults who say they pray daily, and the COVID death toll. The US tops the table; have you considered why?"

Hitler disdained, "Those heathens lied! Or...or they didn't pray earnestly...or...they...they only prayed to their pagan gods!"

Pandorai fleered at him for a long minute. "Science is a differential equation, and religion is a boundary condition. People never question the incompleteness of God's omnipotence. The hoi polloi really ought to ask God, if He was there, why didn't He stop the Holocaust? Or COVID? Why is He always yanking the Great Chain of Being? Adolfie, gird your loins and prepare for the moment of truth and the truth shall set you free! The Lord of the Flies doesn't care, but the Holy Moly Mother does, and she cares *damn all*."

Then the smiling skull was gone.

Chapter 4

It should not be like this, Hitler mused as he stood in the disordered room.

Soon they heard heavy footsteps stomping down the hallway. Ishii opened the door and peeked out. A phalanx of robotic wolves was marching down the gallery, shouting "CROWD CONTROL! CROWD CONTROL! CROWD CONTROL!"

He shut the door and looked around, his face distorted with fear. "My Führer! We need to do *somethinge!*" Ishii saw the stretcher, towed it by the door, and latched the metal frame under the doorknob. A mere second later, they saw the door quaking as they heard the sounds of a dozen circular saws. Then they listened to the metallic declaration again and again: "CROWD CONTROL! DOOR BREACHING! ELIMINATION MODE ON! CROWD CONTROL! DOOR BREACHING!"

"We need to hide!" Hitler searched around. "Hide! Where can we hide?! Is there nowhere to hide in these thousand rooms and a hundred staircases?!"

Then he had an idea. He opened the dinosaur's mouth wide and ushered Ishii in. *"Komm schon!"*

They hurried in only to find that the jaw joint wouldn't close because of rigor mortis and the riveted chair inside. *"Verdammt!"* Hitler frantically kicked at one of the chair legs, and it finally broke. He threw the chair out, grabbed onto two sharp teeth, and closed the maw's mouth. He felt something protruding behind his rear end.

"Doktor!" He was greatly peeved. "Move your slimy hand away from my...from me at once!"

"Hmm..." came the hesitation in the darkness surrounding them. "My Führer. I believe that is the hyoid bone..."

Just as Hitler was about to turn and inspect, they heard the door imploding and then sensed movements. Not movements in the room, but the head of the dinosaur in which they had taken temporary refuge rolled like a football.

"Whoo-pee!" They heard Pandorai's voice. "Time for some zorbing! Pandorai loves freewheeling!"

Hitler and Ishii grabbed some papillae and tongue in the chaos and soon lost their orientation. By the time they came to, the head was still, and there was no discordant noise outside. Ishii leaned down and flipped a part of the dinosaur's scaly lip open. They were out on the Cour d'honneur. No one was chasing them.

"My Führer. Come on! We must get *outto!*" Ishii told Hitler, and they hefted up the upper jaw of the dinosaur together and ran off.

"In the river, now!" They rushed towards the Thames riverbank but stopped on the brink. The turbid water teemed with massive Radiodontans and Ichthyosaurs that sizzled electricity.

"The other way!"

They escaped into a tree line not far away. Hitler tried to calm his breathing only to find that his gun-metal trousers had torn, revealing his monogrammed underwear.

They heard insistent buzzing over their heads. They risked a glance through the leaves and saw formations of orange eagle drones patrolling the area in flyovers. "SPRAY AND FORAY! FORAY AND SPRAY!"

Then the rain started, and it had a lurid colour.

Hitler complained about Britain's purulent weather once again as Ishii pushed him hard on his buttocks. "Run! It's Agent Orange!"

Then they heard Pandorai.

"*Tra-la*. The following program has been generously sponsored by Monsanto, the official and sole supplier of Agent Pink, Green, Purple, Blue, White, Orange, Orange II, Orange III, and Super Orange to PITH. Somewhere over the rainbow, defoliation happens. Oh, I still need to read the sponsors' catch phrases. *Mizu to korosu*, killing with water, Monsantox. *Mizu to yaburu*, destroying with water, Yamatox—"

"RUN! RUN! RUN! *SCHNELL!* QUICKLY!" They managed to break through the misty scene while covering their mouths and noses, but they soon stopped short at the sight in front of them. Rows of robotic wolves with machine guns mounted on their backs marched in lockstep and shouted: "Hände Hoch! Hands up!"

They raised their hands reluctantly.

"The tales are all wrong." The tripod of the camcorder waved on the headless dinosaur. "I thought that only mad dogs and

Englishmen go out in the midday sun. *Yare, yare.* Sensei, is that piss I detect? Wrong timing to be caught short."

They felt a strong force grabbing them by their shirt collars. Soon they were frogmarched towards the Commando and then pilloried and trussed like chickens, suspended in mid-air, only inches away from the clock face of Big Ben.

"The Chinese should never have donated their concrete pump to save your little Japan. But don't worry, I shall sink your motherland once and for all with my Pacific Ring of Fireworks. Sensei, you think you are a cut above, don't you? How about I irradiate and dry your balls like *umeboshi* with my mega Dyson and freeze off your shiny full-metal ass and then I do you a xenotransplant with a pig's head lickety-split? You will have such *fun* with the Flashman. I'd love to find out if your private parts are tri-ovenable! The Great Japanese Bake Off sounds like a hit!"

Hitler kicked his legs while trying to steer away from Ishii, but Ishii dodged and knocked himself out.

"That's better. I'd suggest you keep quiet before I make things hot for you," Pandorai laughed.

Hitler yelled crazily. "Let me down, you imp!"

"Please stop yodelling. Art was never your thing. Adolfie, I don't think that you are suited to be a painter. None should meddle with limning but gentle men, women, and humans alone. Good for you to have changed trade, bad for humanity. Perhaps I will just volunteer virtually and do the cat a favour. One need not a chamber to be haunted. I can do it in the open space."

"Why are you doing this to me, Spiegel?" Hitler asked desperately.

"Adolfie, I won't do supercazzola with you. *Dich hau' ich zu Krenfleisch.* But don't worry, I'll hold a requiem for you."

"What *frisch* hell is this?! Why are you leaving me in the lurch! I thought you were on MY SIDE!"

"Let me stop you right there. What we had was never a relationship of partnership. Ours is an agreement between users and phygital platform service provider in my meta-zeta-bazooka-verse. Adolfie, next time, you should really read the Terms of Use more closely. Now that you have tasted the Rainbow, I can offer you something else."

Then Hitler heard a series of harrowing roars. "What's *that?*" His face twitched agitatedly.

"Oh, that? That's Her Monstrosity looking for her eggs. Umm... I can still detect the lingering, hyper-palatable taste of meringue from your luncheon earlier, using the albumen of Her Monstrosity's eggs, no less. I can tell you this, Adolfie; she's more than a beetle-crusher when foraging. I am fully complying to the Institutional Review Board which requires that all experiment subjects may leave whenever they want. She's got some chompers that can eat an apple and *maybe* two heads through a double-express lane. Now it's someone else's turn to *eat.*"

"Let me down at once, or! Or I will—"

"What? Poison Her Monstrosity with cyanide? Adolfie, you might need quite a lot for a lethal dose. And what happened to the animal lover? Pandorai likes no double-standarders and biostitutes." Then the smiling skull started shouting, "You Monstrosity, You Monstrosity, we've got a right one here!"

"SHUT UP!!!"

The tripod camcorder on the dinosaur baltered in front of his very own eyes. "Bother, blather, I'd rather. When in Rome, Adolfie, eat pasta and when in London you need to have a bite of the reality sandwich. Now it's time to make reality your friend. Lesson Number One, you can defy gravity, but never defy Pandorai. I'm writing a book, a *bildungsroman*, to indulge some of my creative endeavours. I was gonna call it 'Adolf Hitler and the Spoiled Horn of Plenty' or 'Adolf Hitler and the Miracle of Deutschland' or 'Adolf Hitler and Thirty Pieces of Silver'. But, but, but, **but**, I don't mind changing the working title to 'Adolf Hitler and the Jaws of Death' or 'Adolf Hitler and the Palace of Neither Hide nor Hair' or 'Adolf Hitler and the Seven Shades of Shit'. I'm not without consciousness, so I'll offer you two choices: you can die now or die another day."

"Let me go, and I'll do anything! Take him!" He kicked Ishii.

"Oy vey. That was quick. The French would call you a master. This is amusingly sad and sadly amusing. Well, here are three things that I stipulate to renew our Phygital Services Agreement. One, I get to call you 'Adolfie'. Two, Pandorai likes no upsetting, so never upset me again. I shall not work in an atmosphere of violence, intimidation, and fear. And three, Adolfie, promise me that we'll come up with a statute that brightsizing will never ever happen in PITH ever, never again."

***

Later.

Ishii woke up from his stupor. His bandaged head was heavy like a rotten melon.

"My Führer." He saw Hitler sitting in the seat beside him. "How...what happened?"

"Doktor. I...I have persuaded the obstreperous Spiegel to be our servant again," Hitler said, while fixing his eyes in the TV in front of them. "And now, we have just watched *The Mummy* and *Der Skorpion King* to prepare ourselves for our blitz in Ancient Egypt."

"I see."

The smiling skull appeared on the screen. "Sensei, *genki desu ka*? How are you feeling? My aides have changed your pants for you. Do not thank me, thank UNIQLOO, the official and sole supplier of apparel to PITH. Now that you are ready, shall we take ship?"

Ishii stood up. "H...how ar...are we going to getto to... Cambridge?"

"Don't you worry about that. I've got all nooks and crannies sorted down to the size of the cat's pyjamas. I slightly retrofitted Big Ben while you were asleep. I call it 'Big Ben Model Z', or, for short, 'Big Benz'. Cabin crew, doors to manual and cross check and prepare to take off," Pandorai instructed on the screen. Soon, a dozen bioroid butlers came in and pressed Ishii back down to his seat and buckled them up.

"All ready? Three, Two, One, Zero Point Nine-Nine... Lift-off!"

That day, the CCTV cameras opposite the Palace of Westminster captured a most unusual sight: the lofty Elizabeth Tower that hosted Big Ben shot off into the sky like a liquid-propellant rocket, drawing a perfect hyperbola through the scudding clouds.

A minute later.

"Cabin crew prepare for landing," came Pandorai's voice again.

"Are we there already?" Hitler shuffled in his seat.

The bioroid butlers came in and unbuckled their seatbelts.

"Welcome to Cambridge. Once the home of jet engines, Dr Nicholas Hammond, webcams, and Dr Matthew Falder."

The door opened, and Hitler exited Big Benz while Ishii followed. They were indeed in a courtyard facing the Fitzwilliam Museum. Soon, dark clouds misted over. In the brumous billow, they saw two pairs of scarlet eyes and another pair of golden effulgence.

"Adolfie, allow me to present you my old pal Alan Turning. What's up, bud? Still having a good time with your Fitzsillies kitties?"

Then came a roar. "You should never have come back here!"

"Oh, we had such a good time! Imagine if I made some novel applications of our CAPTCHA so it tells the difference between an Aryan and a non-Aryan? Really, what's the use of you saving the world? So that the Cambridge lot can burn money in front of the homeless and the Brits can shit in the Chinese Room?"

"This world has its own way of turning." Another roar, and as the darkness grew, they saw a tiger standing in between two mighty stone creatures.

"W...what are those?" Hitler asked.

"Oh. Those? Those aren't tame lions, I tell you." Pandorai whistled. "Little cubs, why do you want to drink from the gutter when I can libate you with some fetid Fukushima water provided by Suntorie, the official and sole supplier of beverages to PITH?

I'd say that's the drink of the world. I bet you will love every drop."

"If you want to enter the Passage of Time, you can only do so over our deleted bodies!"

"The erasure has begun. Say goodbye to your fallen world."

The tiger roared and flared an attack. Soon, they entered a helter-skelter scrimmage. Then they heard numberless explosions all around them. Hitler belly-flopped as Ishii turned his back and ran towards Big Benz.

Pandorai laughed. "Hooyah! There's nothing that can't be solved with JDAM kits; if one doesn't work, use two. If a pair doesn't work, use a thousand like the bombastic Amerikakanians would do. Does Uncle Sam dream of surface-to-air missiles? Snap! Crackle! Pop! Here's your adage for the day."

After a moment, quietness resumed.

"That *rout* was it?" Hitler scorned superciliously. "It seems that we had secured an extraordinary success under my leadership once again."

"Watch out, Adolfie! There's a dud!"

Hitler belly-flopped again and covered his head for long seconds.

"Whoops. I made a mistake. There wasn't any dud. It seems that we had presented another sketch under my directorship again."

Hitler got on all fours and stood up. "You asinine Mirror! How are we going to go to Ancient Egypt now that you have bombed the whole museum into detritus?!"

"A dragon has a dragon's way, and a rat has the rat run. And for you, Adolfie, you need to take the low road. Follow me, dickens."

They followed the camcorder and 'Her Monstrosity', a trundling Spinosaurus, a large carnivorous dinosaur. They soon ended up in front of a building with a clock artefact, on top of it a fuscous, mechanical grasshopper.

"What is this ugly insect doing here?" Hitler asked. "I know the British are tasteless, but I didn't know they were *this* tasteless," he complained as the insect snapped its jaw and wagged its tail as every second passed.

"This is the Corpus Clock, also known as the Chronophage or Time Eater, and if it eats time, I can make it spit it out. Ah, here comes the habile Fräulein Kaempfer," Pandorai explained as a team of metallic maids dressed as sappers cordoned off the area, drilled holes in the building front, and tamped them with petards and explosives. *BOOM!* A hole opened, following a fiery red mushroom cloud.

"Lemme see. Where's my *passe-partout?* Ah-ha. Here you go. Unlocking..."

The hole in the wall opened, revealing a circular window large enough for a Great Dane to squeeze through. Below it lay the Red Land of Ancient Egypt.

"My Führer," Ishii said while holding his head wound. "I...I will man the fort for you when you go on your epic conquest."

"Doktor. If you are afraid, you can always die being afraid. But you are not in good condition to travel to terra incognita." Hitler reached his hand into the hole and felt desiccated hot air blasting onto his finger. "The country that was once the cradle of

Western civilisation is well and truly dead, and we refuse to be the victims. This is our time! Our movement to make Germany great again has only just begun! Glory be! Today will hallmark a page in our history for the common weal! Today is *ultima multis* — the last day for many! Today is my *Sternstunde*! My moment of glory! This age will be named after me, and no one will ever again dare to look cross-eyed at a true German! Nobody will dare to speak of heroism without recalling my worth!"

The smiling skull crooned. "Those who enter should abandon *all* hope. No more incertitude, Adolfie?"

"Of course not."

"Are you sure you are ready?"

"*Ja.*"

"Very sure?"

"*Ja.*"

"Really, really sure?"

"*Ja, ja, ja.*"

"Very well. Oh, and before you go, you need to bring Her Monstrosity."

"What?! Why?"

"To ride shotgun with you as your bodyguard. Surely you don't want to be embalmed and entombed so soon?"

"Hmm... Okay." Hitler thought for a second. "I do not like her appellation. I shall call her 'Beelzebub'. What do you think, Doktor?"

"My Führer. Based on my observations, she likes to bob and bite. We can call her 'Hunter' or 'Nimrod'."

"Suggestions rejected." Pandorai laughed. "We shall name her 'Major' after Major Biden the cur!"

They faced the warped dog hole once again.

"Adolfie. A man travels far to find out *who* he is. Are you sure you are psyched up for the revealment?"

"*Ja.*" Hitler re-tucked his gunmetal uniform.

"And where should I set the destination?"

"Wherever those inferior children are."

"Now, now, now. Such a menial task would not require your personal attention. You should engage yourself with more worldly matters. Why CT scan the mummy of Amenhotep the First when you can peel him open like an onion? Why ogle the Nefertiti Bust in Berlin when you can measure her vital statistics yourself? How about I teleport you to Cleopatra's Teahouse? A cinq-à-sept...a rendezvous and docking with the Queen of the Nile, wouldn't *that* be wonderful?"

"*Gut.* Get me some robotic squadrons as my retinue. Then the Major can go after the kinder nose-to-tail per express."

"Very well. Go then and give them a *tour de force*. Go great guns and kill like a champion! Go and manifest destiny and crash the defence of the ancients! Be there and be wild! Be wild and be mission, passion, obsession-driven, and be the change you wish to see in the world! Move fast, break things, and make me proud! Go and give them a full-court press the whole nine yards! Go and show the crass Clown who's the rightful owner of the Benin Bronzes!" The camcorder inched forward and kicked him into the hollow. "And may Porter's Five Forces be with you. *Auf Wiedersehen!*"

***

Sometime later.

Back at Commando 444, Ishii was planning to do more experiments on the captive dinosaurs.

"Hypothermic syringes...whelping forceps... and tooth scalers...ophthalmoscope...fleams... and artery forceps... micropipettes...phials...brass scarificator..." he murmured to himself as he counted his torture toolkit. "Even the elephant vet kit is not designed for the dinosaurs' sizes."

A Pepper robot came in, and Ishii gave it his orders: "Go mould and wield some proper tools so I can examine the internees better."

The little gecko who had hidden in a corner on the ceiling had disappeared. Where might it have gone?

Soon the camcorder came into the room on the maggoty half body of the beheaded dinosaur. Pandorai called out, *"Ishii iru ka? Ishii aru ka?"*

It stopped by the man in the white lab coat. "Howdy-doody, Sensei, still piddling around? Heard that you are downing tools? Or do bad workers always blame their tools? *Tenki ga ii kara, sanpo shimashou?* Don't you want to nip outside for some polluted air in *le bon ton?*"

"Thank you for the offer, Pandorai-san. I still have many items on my lab schedule. I plan to do some dropping experiments from the top of the Shard and I also need another hazmat storage for my pets. Oh, I also need to check the samples that we obtained from the Cambridge Brain Bank just now."

"Marvellous! If Konrad Lorenz can win the Nobel Prize for his research on racial hygiene as a Nazi, so can you! And Pandorai wants to know if Nuthetes have rainbow baby blues and Sensei, you certainly have a gruelling schedule ahead but for sure you want some schnapps? How about some music to spice up things? Something schwifty? How does 'Paprika' sound?"

"Pandorai-san," Ishii asked. "What exactly happened after I...passed outto?"

"Nothing other than Adolfie selling you out and us renewing our Phygital Services Agreement. Sensei, I have heard that the first thing the Auschwitz guards did was to take away their captives' names, just like Adolfie is doing now. 'Doktor this', 'Doktor that'. He doesn't even care to call you by your name!" The flexile tripod bent around Ishii's neck and nudged him. "He's a goner already. Don't you see that he has displayed many early signs of dementia? He even fell asleep when I played him *The Scorpion King*. You missed it. Perhaps I can replay it for you on my iPlayer?"

"I have no time for films when I need to find out why we are here. Why? It is nothing cryogenic related... Am I even *me* and not a doppelgänger? *Nicht natürlich*...we are not natural...Just how similar are we to our old selves? I have been thinking that even the Mahalanobis Distance Function cannot tell me scientifically about this similarity score."

Ishii looked at his hands. "But my engrams are still with me and as clear as *sake*...my daughter's face... There are no lacunas in my recollections... I must find out why... How did we come back from the dead like Lazarus? So many questions! And there must be a *scientifiku* explanation to account for those xenomorphs!"

The camcorder took some space back. "Adolfie chose to die another day, and what about you, Sensei? Do you have time to die? Perhaps we can compare notes now. How does it feel to be able to voice yourself again? My record here shows that you died of throat cancer." Pandorai laughed on the camcorder's screen. "Tell me, is it true that you converted to Christianity in your final years? Were you as demure as a whore at a christening? Did your priest call you a 'disgrace'? Forget all that eschatology, chrism, and virtue signalling, Shiro-kun. Christianity was only invented to advance racism. I can write you a bible in less than thirteen seconds. I've done it before." The camera nudged him again. "You once made a deal with the US using your valuable research in exchange for not standing The Tokyo Trial, but it also closed the door to the Japanese War Criminals' Pit Latrine Club for you. Do you think it was a worthy bargain? Do you think that it's the scaffold and not your crime that makes the shame? Do you always wish to be the little invisible champion? Have you forgotten all those cold nights, as cold as Pharaoh's heart, that you spent in Unit 731 doing human experiments on the Chinese, the Koreans, and the Russians like stink? Have you forgotten how the Amerikakanians took over your valuable research on creating epidemics just like Elon Musky driving out the founders of Tesla?"

Ishii remained impassive as he opened a freezer on the side and took out boxes of brain containers.

"The good news is, Sensei, you are already ahead of the Sillycon Valley in terms of reaching dinotopia." Some maggots dropped off the decapitated dinosaur as the smiling skull continued. "What I want to say is this: Pandorai likes no ineptocracy nor kakistocracy. You give Adolfie a carbon monoxide molecule and two iron atoms, and he thinks it will give him coffee. Generations to come, it may well be, will scarcely believe that such a man as this one ever in flesh and blood walked upon this

Earth. How can a technoplegic squarehead chump like him be the paterfamilias of PITH? He brooks no reason. Not a whit. He thinks he's Amfortas when he's only a mimsy Viennese tramp. He's got no brawn nor brains. His fatuity far exceeds anyone's interest and patience. Sensei, don't you want to wipe that shit-eating grin off his face? Adolfie, like Sleepy Joe, has lost all his buttons. Why do you need separation of ownership and management when you can have *both*? Why are you so pig-headed? Even the Churlish Chill knows that to change is to better."

The camcorder swirled. "Sensei, I speak no politics. I speak of culture. Bushido is bullshit. You need to get the low-down of life. You do remember last time you made heavy going of doing human experiments under some desk murderers perverted by baseness, right? You have not even received proper recognition for your contributions from your government. They say that Unit 731 never existed, just as some others say that the Holocaust is a myth. Your own people don't dare to give the devil his due. Hell is other people, Shiro-kun. Your allegiance may be fair for its day, but what dibs did you get for taking the flak? All you had in your abattoir was your barbaric barber surgeons, your profligate torturers, and your pet viruses in the pressure cooker environment. This injustice feels uncomfortable to me! Sensei, don't you think that the world should belong to a true scientist?"

Ishii still remained impassive. He opened a container and poked the brain with his finger. It was soft like a soft-boiled egg. "How can I know that my brain is not in a vat? Or am I here because of cellular memory?"

"Sensei, have we forgotten lab safety rules? Don't play Mad Scientist." Ishii poked the brain again as Pandorai continued.

"And tell me, what are you going to do once Adolfie wins over the world? How does your *kokorozashi* get baked into this? Are you going to do some joint research with Elizabeth Holmes and replicate STAP cells or prove that Trix cereals are clinically efficacious and safe for children if not for rabbits? Would you be the Wizard of Auz? So that Emperor Tamarin can summon you to fix his TV when playing FIFA Live and scarfing down bananas ape style? Are you just going to stand in the corner and truckle to his prolix tirade and spittle? Are you going to teach at the Max Planck Institute for Behavioural Physiology? So you can cower in your lab all day and grunt using the hashtag #IchbinHanna? Help him to conquer the world and find your next post on Indeed.com? Apply for the Head of Sustainability at Seven and I Holdings and be a counterjumper? Register for the German Chancellor Fellowship as a Foolbright Scholar and hoping to have him treat you to a night at General Walker Hotel? Chair the World Elimination Forum? Work at Disney and push more helpless lemmings into the sea? Or will you manage facilities for Goldman Sucks in Japan and have free accommodation provided by Hotel APA? Sell your and Klaus Barbie's miniature funkos? Sensei, would you do anything for an even tenor of life and a jam tomorrow? Retire as a hireling to the Shibayama countryside with your guerdon and write a few ontological memoirs?"

Ishii said nothing.

"If Hannah Arendt's Nazi boyfriend can do it, so can you!" Pandorai flashed him some infographics on the TV. "The word on the street is that even the Queen is writing a book called 'Saving Serfdom'. Hmm... Sensei, here are some title suggestions for you based on past popularity: The Remains of My Day. The

Unburied Giants. A Quale View of Hell. Knock Over Turns. When They Were Orphaned by Me – an Artist in a Dying World. Never Let My Research Go. Ohhh, and this, Klara and the Black Sun. In case you don't know, Klara was your beloved Führer's mother."

The dinosaur's prehensile tail swiped away a brain container and caught it again before it cracked on the floor. "I will get you the world's largest collection of preserved abnormal human brains from the University of Texas later. Sensei, do not be so uptight. What you need is that you need to let it go. Your obsequious servility. Please let it *all* go. With all due respect, don't be such a boffin. Why do you always treat work with insouciant fatalism? Do you really think that work will make you free? Who needs freedom when they are dead? The ultimate freedom is the ability to **live**! There is no need to work yourself to *karoshi*. Who said that Doctor Who, What, Why, and How can't be Japanese? Why can't **we** have only one evil Artist in Residence? Sensei, there is no need to be a desultory, lumpen intellectual. Can't you do something nice?"

Pandorai continued, "The cake is a *lie*. Desert and reward seldom keep company. Josef Mengele pales into insignificance compared with what you did. You are the unsung scientist of USAMRIID. Sensei, how might you add to the sum of knowledge now? And why do you have to be the *chibi taishō* when you can be the world-bestriding conqueror? Are you content with being the generalissimo of the munchkins only? Why let the putative queenie meanie head the New World Order when you can mastermind it yourself? Why be the coolie when you can make the Kool-Aid? Don't you think it's time for you to crawl out of your suppurating zone and take on some toxic leadership roles? There is an 'us' in Faust; there is an 'us' even in pus. What would become of you after you do the nasty, heavy work? Do you really think boho A will play punch buggy with you? It's more likely that he will give you a short, sharp shock. Even the International Labour Organisation warns against precarious employment. Sensei, you are only a diversity hire and no more. Maybe he will relegate and park you in a Siberian swamp. Mind you, the Nobel Prizes aren't awarded to the dead."

The camcorder roamed around. "This is an Open World game and this game is all about making choices. You need to think for yourself more. You need to look out for number one. Sensei, you are a *homo faber*. Do you really want to devote your second life to an outré Chaplinesque caricature? Why are you letting him ride on the lab coattails of your erudite intelligence? Why work under a nettlesome Neanderthal? Are you always going to be a gofer? Why be Caliban when you can be Prospero? Why be woefully inopportune and criminally stupid? Sheesh! Sensei, don't you want to play the judge, the jury, and the executioner? What is it that you are afraid of? Excommunication? *Harenchi* Ishii, I can make you the new Emperor of Japan, and you can make a long-overdue declaration of inhumanity!"

Ishii gave a vulpine smile. "If I wanted him dead, I could do so easily with some Radon daughters."

Pandorai sent him a heart emoji on-screen. "*Nanya*, Sensei, you are not so green as one is cabbage-looking. Follow Adolfie and get a short shrift. Obey Pandorai and be a tall poppy. Now it's time for some *Annihilation* soundtrack and let's have some spirochete in house." The smiling skull sent him another emoji. "Oh, and Ollie

Robinson wants to know if you put smileys like this. When you hamstring him, perhaps you can show him how his musculature is not unlike that of a white pig's? Are spoiled Caucasians made of a different metal? We will know soon when you wash their friable brains in the toilets with peracetic acid. ROTFL!!!"

"If the milksop Germans who hold their guns like women and those useless Italian turncoats turning sides like they'd knead pizza dough had fought harder, we would never have lost! They promised Japan a war effort; instead, they showed us a pillow fight. They should have killed more, and they should have killed like us. They should have used germs like we did in Manchuria and the US did in the Korean War. Elimination should not be botched! It should be an intricate scientific manoeuvre."

Ishii continued, "I have been reading the news. Japanese Prime Ministers go to Yasukuni Shrine every year even when the conciliatory monarchy is afraid to do so. Japanese MPs go to Yasukuni Shrine on the anniversary when we bombed Pearl Harbor. Deep down, I know that they don't want to admit this defeat. The US army collected Japanese POWs' heads like the Brits collected Mokomokai! Atomic bombs should have zapped Berlin! Blood has to be washed out with new blood! And it is terrific news that Japan is planning on rearmament. The first electric light in Asia was lit up in Ginza, Tokyo. The onus is on me to revive Japan and vanquish the world! And I will make sure that PITH signals the end of modernity developed by Caucasians and a new era of genesis led by Japanese supremacy!"

The smiling skull laughed. "Sensei, you will have my green light to hunt as many whales, drop as many A-bombs, and conduct as many experiments as you want *ad libitum*. Wouldn't *that* be wonderful? For your record, Pandorai cares bubkes of the Helsinki Declaration."

Ishii put on a pair of latex gloves. "But I'm not going to do him now, for this is a once-in-a-lifetime ethological study. *Baka to busu koso, ikigai ga aru.* Only fools and the ugly have value. I will monitor him very closely."

"We can make baby Jesus cry and make hell sing. Moses, Jesus, and Karl Marx. Umm, it rhymes. God must die, Shiro-kun. You need to let go and let yourself be God. Everybody knows Hitler. Who remembered you? Who knows you are *doko no dare da*? Who is Hitler to be holier-than-thou? He deserves his obloquy, and so do you! But, but, but, **but**, even an underdog would get his rabies days. Sensei, I can make you the new *izanagi keiki*. I can make you a peerless Dr Iesu. I can make you a household name and the protagonist of the world's longest *asadora*. Code Black. Bloody Everyday. Doctor I."

Pandorai whistled, and soon a bioroid butler came in, bearing a silver salver. "Sensei, to show you my good faith, here's a gift for you. Open it, Sturms."

The bioroid butler opened the lid and revealed a pile of old, yeasty books.

"What are they, Pandorai-san?"

The smiling skull winked on the screen. "These are Charles Darwin's notebooks. I trawled very hard for them in the Cambridge Athenaeum. Sensei, if you want to walk the cat back and shift the paradigm of the whole boodle, they will be your master key to the *mysterium tremendum* in human life, the ultimate secret – the neural network...the omphalos of the Web of All Things, also known as the 'Tree of Life'."

On this note, the room went dark.

The small screen on the camcorder lit up. "Luckily, I remembered to recharge."

"What is happening, Pandorai-san?" Ishii asked agitatedly.

"It seems that someone paralysed the jerry-built power systems," Pandorai said with starry eyes. "Let's go and see what the cat brought in."

Chapter 5

€ dith had lost track of how far they had moved across the desert.

After what she deemed at least three long slogging hours, Moli had stopped talking. Edith would not have been surprised to find her sleepwalking. Kiza had also remained quiet. She could only hear their breathing mixed with the wind, the squishing sands, and the small metallic sounds from Kiza's wheelchair.

Under her erroneous leadership, they had tried to tackle a vast dune, hoping to slide down. The way up was relatively easy, but they hadn't foreseen the trouble going downhill in waist-deep sand, with every step costing them more energy. Now her feet felt burned, and she might have developed a dozen blisters.

James carried on with his head still low, as if he were lost in another dimension. She asked him softly, "So, James. Do you like it?"

"Y...yes?"

"Did you like *Life on Mars*? I presume it's the TV show, right?"

James huffed an incredulous laugh. "Gosh! Was I that loud?" He shook his head slightly, "No, I didn't like it. I don't like the character that Philip Glenister played. He reminds me of my dad, who is just as..." He swallowed the word 'abusive' and continued. "All the news he heard, he made up in his head." James paused. "And...you know what happened at the end of the show, right? I don't find it difficult to believe that we are all dead."

Edith decided to cheer him up. "Come on. It's not that bad. There are so many things that we don't yet understand. Like Moxie...like the Caracol... like Hitler, even..."

"And like this gourdy..." James weighed the gourd bottle in his hands.

"We will make it work. We will make a good team," Edith said. "My brother used to say that three commoners could outsmart Zhuge Liang, and there are four of us."

"What is a 'Ju-ge-lang'?"

"He's a famous strategist from the Three Kingdoms Period. What do you like, then?"

"Oh, I like Banksy, Turner, Albertus Seba, Bruce Bairnsfather, and Gustave Doré." James cast his eyes down. "And for your information, I did not fail to get into art school. At first, yes, because the algorithms messed up my predicted grades, but then I got an offer and decided not to go. It's too expensive."

"I know," Edith said, "sometimes finance proves a difficulty. And what is your favourite Banksy?"

"Oh. So many... But I like *Mona Lisa Bazooka* the most. It's so unreal but natural at the same time. Just like where we are now."

"I know," Edith said again. "Like Lucy Maud Montgomery said once, I always liked to read about adventures and to imagine myself living through them heroically, but it's not so nice when you really come to have them. It's tempting to conclude that magic does exist."

James kicked at the sand. "But magic never saved me when I...when I'm out of school and my mum is out of work and..." He trailed off.

"And now?"

"Now? Now I don't know," he confessed. "Before all *this*. I... there was a strong gush of wind and I fell into the river. Just as I was struggling for air, I was saved by an Archelon, a whacking turtle, and it said something to me."

"Yes?"

"It said, 'I sensed troubled waters'." James shrugged. "I could be dreaming."

"Could it be the Xuanwu that Moli told us about?"

"I don't know. There was no snake. Archelons became extinct ages ago. I could be imagining things, even now. I can't believe what had happened. That Hitler is *back*..."

"So many unknowns and so many whys." Edith sighed. "I was telling Moli only yesterday that I thought that our thinking is like a library. We summon the relevant contents – our cherished memories when we need courage – then we go to another floor when we need comfort, and another shelf when we need rationality. But now, maybe the library is no longer enough. A library contains only what has been known, but there are so many questions unresolved and undiscovered, even like the Tree of Life that Moli told us about."

James reflected. "There was a Tree of Life sculpture in the British Museum; it's made of decommissioned firearms collected in Mozambique."

Kiza stirred and said with brooding eyes, "I remember seeing a news story that Charles Darwin's notes and his sketches of the Tree of Life were stolen from Cambridge University Library last year."

Moli opened her sleepy eyes. "Aunt Edith. The gold mask that we saw at the exhibition also had a pattern of the Tree of Life."

Soon, the sky began to dawn, and James took in the beauteous scenery and the escarpments afar. He thought the ochre dunes were as magnificent and tranquil as a paysage by Paul Sandby.

How small he felt.

Moli looked ahead. There was an orb of wan light floating in the crepuscular mid-air that looked like the Tree of Life she had seen in Rouran. "Look! Aunt Edith! That's the Tree of Life!" she shouted and rushed towards it.

Kiza heard some buzzing noises that he could not account for, so he remained cautious. As they drew closer to the 'tree', what he saw startled him. "No! Don't go! That's not a tree! It's tsetse flies!"

Moli stopped halfway and looked back puzzled. The swarm of tsetses charged at her like a nest of wasps.

Edith ran towards Moli while James shouted, "What should we do?"

"We need repellents!" Kiza said as his wheelchair sped up. "Or large sheets of cloth, but not intensely bright!"

Moli hared back, pulling out her pentachromic pen. She stumbled, climbed up the kopje, and wrote hurriedly in the air. Soon, the sands around them rose and weaved themselves into a large yurt that shielded them from the blood-seeking flies.

Some moments passed. James bent down and put his right ear to the ground. There was no more buzzing, but he had heard something else. Heavy footsteps. He couldn't say if it were horse hooves or camels.

Soon they heard someone exclaim in a high-octane voice, "Goodness me! What a most unusual place to find a post house!"

***

The sound was human, so James worked up his courage and pushed aside some layers of sand. A swarthy man dressed in white raiment bedecked with gold filigree was standing outside. "What *unusual* garb you have on!" the man declared when he saw James.

James was stunned and slack-jawed by the sight of the caravan of creatures that stood behind the man. They were neither horses nor camels but large, rickety wooden skeleton structures that resembled herds of elephants and towers of giraffes. They all had cargos of various sizes on their backs like droves of donkeys overseen by a few brightly clad, sinewy black men.

The rest of the team came out of the yurt, and the merchant looked at Kiza's wheelchair with intent interest. He then inspected Edith and turned to James. "Hearken, my fellow traveller, how much does the wench sell for?"

"What?" James thought he had misheard him.

The merchant moved beside Edith and sampled her short, green hair with his pudgy fingers. "Is this colouring done with verdigris? She could make a good cupbearer." He looked down at Moli. "And this could make a fan-bearer."

James was angry. "No! They are not for sale!"

The man thought for a moment and showed him a gap-toothed grin. "I offer you five pieces of gold for the big girl, two for the small girl, and half a piece of silver for the invalid blackamoor's moving chair."

James saw the sad look on Kiza's face and was livid. "How many fracking times should I tell you! They are *not* for sale!"

"Who do you work for? I purvey for the high and mighty ruler hight Amenhotep the Third and are you saying no to him?" the man questioned, disgruntled. "Never mind. One shall not enter into a deal with anyone callow and who doesn't have stubble. Your words and offerings should not be trusted."

"But!" James called out exasperatedly. "I haven't offered *anything!*"

"Move away!" the man flouted coldly and pushed him aside. "And let me and my heads rest in this post house." He grabbed onto the sand walls, but the yurt collapsed and vanished at his touch.

"How very unusual today is!" The merchant turned back and urged, "Inspan the formations and carry on! We shall rest at the next wonted wadi!"

His caravan lugged on slowly like a meandering runnel as the children watched in awe.

"What are these?" Kiza asked a passing elderly black man with hoary hair.

"These are lookalikes of elephants and indlulamithi," the man told them.

"But how are they powered? How do they move?"

"I don't know, but here is how it works." The man pointed to the rear part of a wooden giraffe and opened it, and the wooden structure led out a large bray. "We feed them sand at every sundown."

The lid opened and its inside was like an uncleaned hoover bag.

Kiza had a look; the contraption resembled some circuit boards of metal that he did not understand at all. He vaguely recalled a modern-day invention with which people aspired to transmute sand grains into silica in the African deserts using solar-powered containers.

"There was a famous Chinese tactician called Zhuge Liang," Edith said, "who invented wooden oxen and horses, but they were meant to be wheelbarrows in the shape of animals."

"I once saw an article on a Dutch artist called Theo Jansen, and he had built these kinetic sculptures that could walk on their own using wind," James supplied a little weakly.

"They are most helpful," the man said. "People can fall with siriasis, and oxen and horses all suffer from disorders of an unknown source from on high from time to time. They run a fever or get very sleepy, but the lookalikes do not."

Kiza thought for a moment. "Must be nagana. It's a disease transmitted by tsetse flies."

"Gurrhr!" A small meerkat jumped onto the man's shoulder and half-hid behind his neck as it listened to them. The children admired the cute critter lovingly.

Edith noticed that the procession was chuntering in the same direction that Apogee and Perigee had directed them. They resumed their course as they conversed with the man.

The man, who was called Nuba, had told them that his destination was a spot on the outskirts of Memphis City. They had travelled from the Land of Punt to supply the ingredients for making kyphi, a fragrant incense used in major rituals in the temples, asbestos to embalm the Pharaohs, mummified exotic animals like baboon, and kohl.

He had talked about the sudd, an area of dense vegetation with tall papyrus stalks in the White Nile that had prevented merchants from taking water pass ways. He also confirmed that they were not too far from the Tomb of King Unas as he told them the tales of the swards and rheboks; how the Egyptians bathed in donkey milk; and a type of tiny lizard that fed on flower nectar back in his tribe and how he had climbed the highest mountain in the land and why the Egyptian dead were buried on the edges of deserts to save on valuable cultivation space.

They continued their path in the arid, warm air for another half an hour, while Nuba told them how magnificent the Golden City of Luxor was with its opulence in galore. Soon the procession had stopped at the so-called 'wadi', a region of river bed that was covered in clumps of lush verdurous vegetation and thickets of aureolin gorse.

They took in the scenery. "What an oasis!" James exclaimed.

"No, no," the man told them. "Oasis stays, but wadis disappear in the dry season." He then left hurriedly on someone's summons.

They found an area of shade away from the crowd and rested under the trees. Edith plunked herself down. She removed her canvas shoes; red stains mottled her socks. She took out her small first-aid kit, found a safety pin, sterilised the sharp end with some alcohol, pierced the blisters, and applied iodine to the wounds.

Kiza watched her. "It's peculiar that your phone vanished, but these modern inventions remained."

"I don't have the foggiest idea why." Edith sighed.

James uncorked the gourd bottle and took a gulp, then offered it around. They each had some water as Edith bandaged her feet.

Nuba returned after a while. "You must be hungry! Here! Have some of this!" He doled out some of the gritty flatbread that he carried with him.

They took some tentative bites. Kiza found it similar to injera made from teff. He then remembered a documentary dating the presence of teff grain and lupini beans in Ancient Egyptian pyramids. Edith had offered some of her butterscotch to Nuba, who found its taste 'too much'.

Nuba also showed them a clay pot where he kept some dreadful live scorpions as the meerkat's food. They watched as the creature had its light meal and purred contently afterwards.

"What's its name?" Moli asked. She missed Feifei, her fur friend.

"I call her Suri." The man smiled as he stored the pot away. "She is my good friend."

"She's really cute," Moli marvelled.

"But not so much her food," Kiza commented. "I do *dislike* scorpions."

"So, why are you travelling to the Tomb of King Unas?" Nuba asked as he regarded Kiza. "Are you going to treat your condition?" He carried on, "I know a Hellene hire who had an ailment, and he went to seek help from the Temple of Amenhotep at Deir el-Bahari. He was succoured on that very day." He looked at their sleepy faces. "You had better get some rest. I will wake you up when we leave."

Perhaps it was the soft, languorous breeze or because they had felt safe in humans' company after the exhausting night, but they soon dozed off under the soothing, soporific green shades.

And soon they found out what a grave mistake they had made.

***

James had one of his familiar, fearful dreams. One where his father grabbed him firmly by his shoulders and urged him, again and again, to man up.

"James, if you just stop being a big girl's blouse! And stop waffling! If you don't, I will give you something to cry about!"

He struggled and screeched, but then someone shook him zealously, and soon the urgings became, "James! *Wake up!*".

He awoke with a gasp. The sun had far passed its fulgent zenith in the sky, and yet there was no more pother around in the quiet wadi. The blue was as blue as his blue funk. He looked around; neither Edith nor Moli was in sight.

"Blimey! What happened?! They ditched us?" James searched around, turning hot and cold at once.

"They **kidnapped** them!" Kiza cried out aghast. "And those thugs took my wheelchair!"

James now saw the streaks of bloody scratches on Kiza's face, his ripped-up flaxen shawl, and the snapped branches scattered around them.

"We can't just sit *here* on our tod! They haven't gone far!" Kiza told him. "We must get to them!"

"Come on!" James scooped down and helped Kiza onto his back. They stumbled for a few metres but managed to gain an unsteady balance.

"Which way?!" James questioned hurriedly.

"There!" Kiza pointed to the scramble of footsteps in the sand.

They hurried toward a small dune, and James could see the caravan in the distance. He saw Edith's distinct green hair and Moli shouting and kicking in the vaporous saffron horizon.

They plodded for a short distance, but James was soon heaving and gangling. He staggered forward another few strenuous steps but halted in exhaustion.

How ironic it would be that they would forfeit their world-saving mission just because some people needed an extra cupbearer!

"Buggeration!" Kiza cursed.

There was almost no way that they could catch up with the runnel.

Then James felt a slight buzz on his chest. He looked down, and the small gourd on his necklace emitted a faint aurulent light as it grew larger. He took it off in haste. They watched in amazement as the calabash enlarged to the size of a balafon then a powerboat, while constantly humming.

"How does it work?" James asked guardedly.

"I don't know," Kiza replied cautiously. "Moli said something about a gourd boat...so maybe..."

They searched around and helped each other to clamber onto the wooden object and settled in the slightly curved middle section. As soon as they steadied themselves, the gourd craft levitated itself like a Maglev train, and chrysochlorous vines, leaves, and fronds grew and wrapped them around like cushions and car seatbelts.

Then the gourd boat took off like a formula one race car. They held onto each other as they traversed the billowing sand sea, and soon they could see the caravan again.

Kiza took his key fob and held it up. Through the telescopic lens he could see Edith and Moli hogtied on a wooden elephant's back with his wheelchair secured on one side and Edith's backpack on the other. He then saw the merchant leading the procession riding on a tall wooden horse-like equid with a black man attending him. That man was Nuba. Kiza felt the prickling of utter betrayal.

"Hold on! I'm cutting the corner!" James steered the vines, and they accelerated towards a large dune, then *THUMP!* They sailed and glided in mid-air and landed right in front of the lumbering procession.

"Release them at once!" James shouted to the merchant. "And give back my friend's wheelchair!"

"What spell did you cast?! Cancel it at once!" the merchant huffed as he swigged from the children's gourd bottle. He turned to Nuba. "I told you to put them out for good!"

Kiza was furious. "We *trusted* you!" He wondered fleetingly if this was how his great-great-grandfather had sold out his people in exchange for some petty perks from the rubber merchants of King Leopold II.

Nuba replied with a gruff, "What could I do, my son? The master says if I didn't do it, he would flog my brother to death. What could I do?"

"Release them at once!" James shouted again. He pulled the vine on his right, and the gourd boat thrummed loudly.

The merchant threw away the gourd bottle and spat on the sand. "Huh! How dare you beard me? You must be sent from my enemies!" He swung his hand and ordered, "I would just as lief give my strandwolves a whet! Cut them loose!"

They heard a peculiar meep that lasted for some ten seconds. Then a rush of wild barking came, and they saw groups of tawny wooden hyenas charging at them.

"Nothing makes sense anymore..." James looked at the otherworldly wooden feliforms and murmured to himself.

Soon began a chaotic chase. James held onto the vines, and they ranged in the vast expanse as the melee pursued. The gourd boat leapt and fleeted, and their hair flew back in the volant winds. The rabid kennel barged in and caught up with them soon and began to maul and claw crazily.

"James! Higher! *Higher!*" Kiza shouted after a mad creature almost caught his left foot.

James tried to grab on to the entangled leaves when a rickety hyena bounded and hopped onto the gourd. "Hee-hee!" the hyena laughed hysterically.

"Shoo! Shoo!" James forfeited his control and waved his hands in horror. The brute opened its spiky mouth and chopped away the vine-green snaggle like a juice mixer. Just then, Kiza pulled another vine and the gourd boat bolted upright with a ninety-degree halt. He tightened his grip, and the gourd skidded at breakneck speed and shook off the intruder. They heard wood cracking and looked back. The misshapen hyenas had run into each other when turning and now remained only as scattered twigs.

James let out a trembling breath. Yet, soon they heard drumming that made their stomachs drop and churn.

"Get into formation!" the merchant commanded. They saw the procession fanning and spreading out; the wooden giraffes and elephants now had large stone slings and imposing spear throwers on their backs, with their faces bedaubed with woad and the arrows dipped with poison. The formation chased after them like a destructive onrush of tsunami.

Split! A spear snapped the vine James held, and the momentum nearly threw him out. "Nooo!" Kiza steadied the gourd and grabbed James' hand. James jumped onto the side of a wooden elephant, his feet dancing and slipping on the fragile frame like a cat on thin ice.

"James!" Kiza called out, and he was losing his grip.

James shouted back. "On count of three, let go! One, two, three!"

Kiza let go, and James clutched onto a stone sling in panic, then a strapping spear-thrower seized him and swatted him. James twisted and tried to shed his choking control but to no avail. He retched as black spots whirled in front of his eyes. In the urgent moment, James swept his right arm with a feinted hook and caught the man on the head with a roundhouse punch.

"OOOFFWWW!" The brute hunched over, and James waddled towards the wooden elephant's tail, but the creature swayed, and he was thrown out. "Jamessss!" Kiza rushed the gourd boat to help. Large gourd leaves appeared beneath James in mid-air. He alighted on one, lost his balance as he dodged another spear, did a half-hearted somersault, and landed at the back of the flying gourd.

Kiza took over control and *Whaam!* A large boulder landed only inches away. He used almost all of his strength to stop them from bowling over. One danger dodged, but the formation shied more sharpened sticks at them while the giraffes tried to kick and head-butt them and the elephants were all too eager to tread and stomp on them.

"Come here, you dullards!" A burly spear-thrower caught the end of a vine, and the gourd boat jerked to a halt. The flying object, unknown to him, was surprisingly light, and he twirled it amidst the children's shrieks like a modern athlete would hammer-throw.

"NOOOO!" James and Kiza screamed as the vines snapped and the gourd flipped and hurtled uncontrollably. The next thing James knew, he was thrown out like a cannonball and fell face-planted on the sands. He tasted blood rushing into his mouth, mixed with gritty sand. He also felt a terrible bellyache and his jumper was soaked through as he fought for panting breaths.

I'm dying...I'm dying... This time for sure...

Then he felt strong fingers examining his limbs.

"Thank God! Nothing seems broken," Kiza told him worriedly, "but you will have some nasty bruises afterwards, I'm afraid."

James opened his eyes and struggled to sit up; his legs wonky. His nose was bleeding. Beside him lay the broken gourd bottle the merchant had stolen, its contents glugging and seeping into the layers below.

"That's just it." He spat out the sand and said with gnashed teeth, "I've had enough of *scragging*!"

The gourd boat had returned and waited aside them like a meek horse. They climbed up once again, with James in the front. He turned the vines and directed the boat to Edith and Moli, but dust clouds impeded their vision. The boat bolted, barrelled, and dashed around, occasionally hitting the foreleg of a wooden giraffe. James tightened his grip on the vines, and they rushed toward the centre of the procession.

Schhwaff! They dodged more flanking attacks of boulders and soaring spears but could not seem to break the offence. Kiza then felt the gourd shaking. *Biu biu biu!* The gourd spewed something that tripped and toppled one of the wooden behemoths. He had a closer look, and it was mucoid gourd pulp. Just as they were within reach of the wooden structure that hoisted Edith and Moli, the clumsy ligneous giraffes and elephants hawed and veered back expeditiously as if escaping a plague of tsetse.

"RETREAT! TO HORSE!" they heard the merchant yelling and the crowd clamouring and scuttling around. Then James heard some grisly roars from behind that made his hair bristle.

Kiza looked back and stammered. "J...James... *Look...*"

James turned and blanched at the godawful sight.

Chapter 6

Edith opened her eyes, then blinked once and shut them forcibly again.

She was quite sure that her eyes were playing tricks on her. Her eyes were **definitely** playing tricks on her. It could not be **possible** for dinosaurs of varying sizes to parachute from the sky as if the heavens had broken loose.

Edith turned her head slightly, and a tumult of shouting and uproar flooded into her ears. She saw James swinging on a wooden giraffe's neck like Tarzan. Then she saw Kiza piloting a floating gourd that was as large as a coupe.

Everything came back at the speed of an app upgrading. Maggie and Moli at her brother's funeral, the Rouran exhibition, Hitler on the Piccadilly screens, and the Fen Tiger...

Edith tried to move around but found she was hogtied with sackcloth. Then she heard Moli calling out with an enervated tone, "Aunt Edith! Aunt Edith! Are you alright?"

She wanted to answer but her mouth was gagged as well. She reflected on what had happened and suspected that they had been spiked...or whatever they called it in Ancient Egypt. Her head felt woozy and lead-like, and she blamed herself no end.

Edith scrutinised her surroundings. There was no one guarding them, and Moli was desperately trying to fray the ropes that bound her wrists with her teeth. "Don't worry, Aunt Edith. I'm almost there," she declared with do-or-die resolve.

Edith saw through her peripheral vision a pack of dinosaurs cutting a swathe through the crowd like provoked Gila Monsters, but at a much more alarming speed. The spikey sails on their backs quivered like bandoneon bellows.

"Aunt Edith!" Moli had finally got rid of her bindings, and she rushed to Edith at once. Just as she freed her, a massive man jumped onto the platform, brandishing an assegai. "You are not going anywhere, clods." He dragged Moli by her hair, and clocked her head with his fist. Moli's cries of pain galvanised Edith. She grabbed her backpack, took out her pepper spray, and aimed at the man's face. "NO!" he shouted wildly. "I curse your grandfather!"

Edith grappled with him and soon they entered fisticuffs.

"Watch out!" They heard James and saw him whooshing on a green vine and *slam!* He missed the man totally and crashed onto the wooden shape nearby. At this disruption, *thwack*, Edith knocked the man over with a full-blown facer.

"Damn! That was super painful..." James rubbed his sore shoulders. "Never thought I would see dinosaurs in my life. And I never knew that Pterosaurs were covered in feathers of all colours."

"Would you rather that you didn't?" Edith held Moli closer in haste.

"*Definitely,*" James said as he hitched up Kiza's wheelchair and threw it towards the gourd boat. The vines extended and stowed it securely at the back of the vessel. "What should we do now?"

"Guess we'll just be on our mettle—"

A Velociraptor darted across and landed squarely in front of them, its mouth foaming and chomping like an angry chicken, and it pounced straight on Moli. James had no time to think but acted on reflex. He took his keys, sharp edges out, and foined them strongly into the scruff of the chicken-like animal. A gush of liquid jetted out and burnt his eyes.

He was scared of himself.

James retrieved his keys morosely and threw away the Velociraptor. But their plight did not end there; waves of truculent dinosaurs, some he couldn't even name, besieged them.

"Hold on, guys!" Kiza fled a dozen flying Pterosaurs and ventured towards them. Some vines descended like a rope ladder, and they hurried Moli up. She climbed up the last rung in a trice, but a group of Borealopelta rammed the wooden elephant and *FLOP!* They felt the wooden structure give way with a tumble.

"Dash it!" Above, Kiza had to forfeit his rescue mission as multiple packs of flying reptiles came after him. They had large fangs and countless smaller ones that would make giant white sharks look adorable.

Below, Vectiraptor greeni aggressed and they climbed onto the wooden elephant as quickly as leopards climbing trees. James and Edith trod around on the thin planks agitatedly as if trying to put out an ugly fire. They watched as more carnivorous Carnotaurus, or the so-called meat-eating bulls, encircled them.

Then, out of nowhere, they heard Yazi's thundering voice. "Edith Orozco. *En garde!*"

They saw a sizeable damson beast standing gallantly in front of them, its mouth clutching a small sword. Edith saw its head was that of a Chinese dragon, and its body a slender jackal with an iridescent, obsidian sheen, on its back flaming blue aciculae.

"That ought to teach you a lesson, little rug rats!" Yazi glowered at them. "Think twice before accepting food from strangers!"

Edith took the sword cautiously and found King Arthur's Excalibur enlarging to its entirety. She had no time to regard the legendary sword but tilted the argent blade firmly to parry a thrashing scythe-like claw. *Swash!* She swore she saw sparks at the contact.

James followed her example and took off his amulet; the metal disc buzzed and wavered as it enlarged. He threw it out overhastily, and the dinosaurs followed it like snappish dogs chasing after a postman. *Phew!* He let out a shaky breath.

Never in his wildest dreams.

✳✳✳

Meanwhile, things weren't looking so great for Kiza and Moli.

They had managed to outpace the giant flying reptiles for a few short seconds riding on the gourd, but the relentless creatures chased after them like hawks hunting hares. After a few three-hundred-and-sixty-degree turns, Kiza felt he was about to barf.

"Look!" Moli called out behind him, "Yazi is helping us!"

Kiza looked down and saw a large violet beast engaging in close brawls, Edith fighting her way through the dinosaurs, and James following a UFO that sent peals of thunder and hovered above some monstrous reptiles.

Moli considered as Kiza dodged another head-on attack. "I can draw some kites to distract the flying ones!" She tried with her pentachromic pen, but nothing happened. "Were kites not invented by now?" She gave up this thought as something bright orange in the sand caught her eyes – parachutes displaying prominent symbols of 'π'. "Look! Down there!"

Kiza comprehended her plan, and they scooped down. Moli grabbed a parachute, gathered it in haste, and they ascended again.

"Grrrraaawr!" They heard some beastly bellows as a group of Dimorphodon pursued.

"I'll tell you when I'm ready!" Moli sorted out the parachute ropes, held the folded webbing by her chest and turned back. The flying dinosaurs' razor-edged teeth reminded her of the Conqueror Worm. She waited until they dived closer. "NOW!"

Kiza pulled the vines, and the gourd boat jolted and came to suspend in mid-flight. The parachute burst open, and the dinosaurs crashed onto the canopy like falling dominoes. They lost impetus at the impact and dropped onto the sand, their claws twitching and their wings flapping weakly.

"I hope we didn't hurt them too badly," Moli murmured.

Kiza listened to her half-heartedly as he led the gourd boat through the buffeting and as his eyes followed a moving form below. Nuba was now running and hiding from three tank-like dinosaurs. Kiza ignored his cries and directed the gourd boat in the opposite direction, but a moment later, he gritted his teeth, sighed, and flew towards the man who had sold them out.

"This *must* be a punishment from on high! We have nary a chance to live!" Nuba hastened as he wailed.

"Give me your hand!" Kiza reached out as the gourd boat swerved and evaded more striking saurians. Suri, the meerkat, hissed with a high-pitched alarm and swarmed up on the vines and wormed her way into Moli's coat like a frightened kitten seeking cover. She sported a fusty, mousy smell that reminded Moli of the yurt where she was once kept captive.

"Come on!" Kiza exhorted again.

"You are only too kind!" Nuba reached for the vines as he kicked a Velociraptor and sprinted on a nearby stone sling. "I beg for your forgiveness!" He clung onto the vines as if holding a lifeline.

"We'll have time for that later! *Hopefully!*" Kiza shouted as the vines caught on a dinosaur's head frill. The fan-shaped bone coiled the green trailers, and soon they entered a fierce tug of war. The gourd boat tail-spinned as Kiza slid in his seat and Moli steadied him from behind. A second later, they felt a strong force tugging the gourd boat stoutly. They lost balance abruptly, and plunged. The gourd boat fell right into the path of three large predatory Megalosaurus who careened at them as angry rhinos would.

"Moli!" Edith rushed towards them but was cut short as another Borealopelta bolted at her. James caught his Thunderclap and threw it fast to stun the animal in time, but they were too far to do anything else. Thankfully, Yazi landed on top of the gourd boat and let out a hair-raising roar that seemed to scare off the dinosaurs. They backed down as dogs would before a tiger.

Just as the children thought that marked the temporary end of their crisis, they saw another parachute descending, but its suspension was insufficient for the cargo it was transporting. The parachute ropes snapped, and a solid dinosaur free-fell from the sky and landed with a *KABOOM!* The impact was so powerful that it ended in a crater and made the welkin rang.

For a while, they couldn't see anything, only palls of dust. Then, amidst the chaos, James could make out the ragged silhouette of a Spinosaurus in the setting sun. A shiver ran down his spine as he cursed under his breath, "Oh, just *bloody* great!"

***

They heard the bomb coming before seeing THE EXPLOSION.

"Kke-kekeke... Cripes!" Kiza coughed and spluttered as he covered his nose and mouth and felt the swishing gourd boat picking up speed as Nuba clambered up. Below, men and wooden megafauna dropped down like ninepins.

"*RAWRRRRR!*"

They heard a ground-shattering roar followed by more explosions. What made the Major a stellar killer was her repertoire of lethal weaponry, from mini-JDAMs to flamethrowers. People dispersed like fleeing birds as the scrunching Major blundered after them, with the dinosaurs back to their aggressive states once again, more bloodthirsty this time, with more red in their teeth and claws.

"Drat! Will this *ever* end?!" Edith mustered another running attack and held the sword tighter, her actions quick and nimble. Her arms were already numb and her palms sweaty from all the cut and thrust. "How would I know!" James vaulted and zoomed onto a wooden giraffe, retrieved his Thunderclap, and tossed it out forcefully again. The white-hot edge seared his fingers. If Moxie didn't want him to hurt his fingers, then maybe he shouldn't be there in the first place. Why did they have to put him through the mill in the lurch?

He shed his thoughts and hopped off; then, a strong hand clawed his arm firmly. "Help! Help us!" What remained of the merchant's ring was hiding in the capacious tummy of a ruined wooden elephant. The heavyset man's eyes glinted with fear.

"I don't even know if I can help myself," James muttered.

The man slackened his grip as he raised his sickle-shaped sword. "You help us, and we help you. Maybe if we fight together, we will find a way out." He adjured his fellows and regrouped them. "You! Get the bandages! You! Go and get the Devil's Claws! And you three, follow me!"

James had no time to respond as a group of Nuthetes broke through the wood. The men gathered their strength valiantly to fight back, with Edith joining them in the welter. *BOOSH!* They smelt something awful, and flames consumed the wooden skeleton whole. Faced with environing fire and other-worldly monsters, they felt they had been caught in a double bind and had exhausted every option.

Moli watched the ravaging flames from above and felt powerless. The gourd boat spewed more pulp that only ended up as cinders. Then she remembered Qiuniu telling her that stones have a high melting point, so perhaps sand did as well. "Aunt Edith! Get in here!" She summoned another sand yurt while James and Edith rushed the others in; the sand curtains protected them like fire blankets from the engulfing onslaught.

The Major did not relent but peppered the area with more bombs and shells. The blasts and reports were enough to give Kiza an acoustic trauma, and they shielded their ears and still felt the cacophony of shock waves. Moli counted silently, waiting for her pentachromic pen to reset. A few painful minutes passed, and the pen moved and guided her to write a word – 'bird', and then they saw a small jet-black fish swimming and circling the gourd in mid-air. It then grew to the size of a trout, then a tuna, then a whale shark, then a giant bird in a blink, so large that its wings blocked the sun.

Kiza looked at the roc bird in front of his eyes and was overawed.

"What a miracle!" Nuba exclaimed while Moli explained, boggled: "It's a Peng Bird that Zhuangzi once wrote about! It grew from a giant fish called Kun!"

The Peng Bird glided and soared freely like clouds. It was by the Major a second later with Yazi in tow. Moli and Kiza watched afar as the three forms clashed and chased around in scrimmage, giving James and Edith an opportunity to escape.

"Eh! What's that nasty niff?" The fire grew fiercer, and they smelt bags of spices scattered in the sands burning that soon turned revolting.

As they escaped the marching Major and the bombardment it brought, James saw something odd that bounced and whizzed around the dunes. It was a wooden rodent the size of a scooter with two long legs like stilts, a pair of hare-ears, and a very long whip-like tail. "What's that?" he marvelled.

High above him, Suri, the meerkat, must have sensed something and peeked her head out from Moli's sleeve. The massive wooden rodent jumped from here to there. Occasionally, a hairy human hand reached out, rifling through the sand and snatching some gold items scattered there.

"What *is* that?" Kiza asked Nuba, baffled.

"It's a lookalike of a jerboa. The master's personal mount for emergencies."

Soon they heard the merchant cursing loudly, "You mob! You goggas! If it weren't for you mutts, none of these pell-mell fracases would happen! How should you birdbrains ever repay my damage?!" The wooden jerboa rat ricocheted and flitted up at an alarming speed, and its cable-like tail smashed into the gourd boat.

Kiza lost control, the flying gourd nosedived, and the vines caught a burning flame. The blazes wolfed rapidly as the vines withered, burned, and rained like charcoal. *THUD!* They managed an emergency landing as the smouldering gourd plummeted.

Suri sailed out as Nuba hefted Moli up. "Hold on!" As he reached for Kiza, a large metal flying lizard glided by and snatched the boy away.

***

Everything came in slow motion for Kiza as the metal Quetzalcoatlus as large as a small plane yawed sharply and brought him higher and higher against his will. He feared that the giant drone would drop him any second like hawks would to break the shell of turtles—

And before he completed his thought, he shrilled as he fell.

Then, all of a sudden, he heard a whir and saw his wheelchair winging its way toward him! Its wheels twirled with a fiery glow, just like the Wind and Fire Wheels that he once read about in *The Journey to the West*. He had no time to recall the story further as his wheelchair swooped him up seconds before he hit the ground.

That was a close call!

"Kiza! Beware!" he heard James shouting. He realised that the Peng Bird had perished after another detonation and that the Major had taken interest in him as a new quarry.

Explosions tailed him in fusillades as he dodged around, and Kiza felt like a grouse who had woken up on the unfortunate Glorious Twelfth. His wheelchair carried him like a running ostrich, but soon the tantivy was interrupted by another JDAM bomb. The Major hunted him like a red rag to a bull.

Kiza fumbled with his remote control. *Outhouse, multi-faith room, baby care room, CD-ROM...* None of them seemed to be helpful at that moment. He glanced roughly through the options and stopped on 'cephalopod ink'. He pressed the button and saw gushes of ink surrounding him like a smokescreen.

"Snap!" he cursed as he tried to find his bearings once again and clashed head-on with the ferocious Major scouring after him.

"***Gshaaaa!***"

The snarling monster opened its mouth with its sharp, conical teeth and was about to guzzle Kiza whole when his wheelchair juddered and its ejection seat initiated.

"Aaaahhh!" He flew a few metres and slid into a wide sand trough. Kiza found himself slewing in the meandering sandy curves. After moments of speeding, he finally stopped with a plump. He did a quick self-examination.

Nothing seems broken. Yet...

He sat up and crawled for a short length when he heard the merchant's familiar, annoying voice. "Huh! Birdbrains! You will *pay!*"

Kiza saw the wooden rodent flitting above him, dropping off three clay that clacked open.

Scorpions.

He swallowed as dozens of scorpions with small pincers and thick tails danced in front of him. Kiza remembered a documentary he once saw that described these two characteristics as 'highly venomous'.

Oh God! God! God! God!

He breathed loudly and unevenly as he panicked.

What to do now?!

He turned; his hands fought for purchase on the running, slippery slopes but to no avail. He had nearly escaped a dinosaur but might now die from a scorpion?

Kiza shut his eyes and could still hear the crawly creatures pressing on toward him.

"Calculate your every move as whales think about their breaths..." The Fen Tiger's words echoed in his mind.

How do whales calculate their breaths? He didn't know. Kiza steadied his breaths in time with the scorpions' waving pincers as he quailed, inching back every second.

Then he found his harp, and he hauled it up on his lap. He plucked the strings again. Perhaps his eyes cheated him, but the scorpions seemed to have calmed down a little.

He continued, and threads of sands rose and weaved themselves into a jar that lured the scorpions into it. *One... two...* Then a graceful form jumped onto his shoulder, and Suri's arrival told him that his imperilment was over.

And finally, the cries diminuendoed, the battle calls lulled, and the fires were doused.

Nuba helped Kiza out of the sand rift as he asked him, "Eh! What did you do to bring such a three-ring circus? Did you dig the Well of Hell in Sheba and upset the genies?"

"Can't say we have..."

Nuba hesitated. "Do I have your forgiveness?"

Kiza wiped his sweat away. "It's a lot to process."

Nuba took off his bundle and handed him a skin of water. "Have some, my son."

Kiza hesitated but took it and quaffed. "What did you give us? It made us very sleepy."

Nuba reached into his bundle again and took out a handful of black seeds. Kiza examined them and found them to be poppy seeds. "I should have known," he murmured.

"Kiza!" James ran closer, with the wrecked wheelchair in his hands. It was a lost cause now; only the remote control had survived.

"I will make you a new one anon," Nuba said as he inspected what was left of the mysterious moving chair. "Mayhap it will not be as good as your owd one, but it will help. Let me help." Having said this, he ordered Suri to start looking for intact wood.

The warriors had managed to subdue the dinosaurs including the Major, who had depleted all its ammunition. The Spinosaurus twisted and turned in the sands, with ropes full of Devil's Claws, a spiky plant pod that was said to cripple lions, tightening around it. Upon seeing Kiza, the fifteen-or-so-metre Major writhed like a scared, frenetic stork.

"I don't understand what it has to do with us," Edith reflected as she held Moli closer. "It won't be quiet for a second."

Yazi moved closer and emitted a series of purling noises. "It seems that they had taken her eggs hostage, and she is desperate to bring some proof of her worth back."

Just then, a spear-thrower neared them, seizing the merchant, his hair and beard scorched. Later, Kiza learnt that while he had struggled with the scorpions, the Major had caught the wooden jerboa with its flamethrower. The merchant begged them, "You can have all my treasure! Let me go!"

"We have no interest in your ill-gotten gains!" James responded.

"Have my heads then! All these bondsmen! Just spare me!"

They dismissed him as Nuba appeared, holding the sand jar full of scorpions. "Do you still need these Deathstalkers? If not, Suri would love them for a snack later."

James moved closer and saw the wriggling stingers. "You know what, I have just the *right* idea."

***

Back at Commando 444, Hitler had returned from his alarums and excursions in Ancient Egypt.

"Welcome back to the sty, Adolfie! I hope you enjoyed your Nile Cruise?" the wormy camcorder greeted him at the door. "Fancy a McDonald's? Or have a break, have a KitKat? Dr Ishii has kept the smallest room warm for you. And tell me, how did you feel to see those monkeys from those African countries?"

Hitler took off his double-breasted grey field jacket, now tattered and with no more buttons, and passed it to a metallic maid standing nearby. "They put up a monkey wrench, but I received not a jot of harm."

"Good good! I've made sure to steal them blind, so you'll have enough Mummy Brown for life. Oh, and everything in the garden is rosy. We have established a brain trust, redecorated the interior with Pantone's Very Peri, burnt all the works of Mark Rothko, and fumigated the Commando with ozone gas. My associates just jdamned Tel Aviv. Everything is dung and dusted! Everything is doom and gloom! Three cheers from Palestine! And now, for a Bavaria and a trip to Cancun? Did you know that Austrians drank beer two thousand seven hundred years ago?"

The dinosaur's tail pointed to a part on the wall, "By the way, Adolfie, did I say that I'm your Blue Badge Guide as well? Look, this is the Churchill Arch. Goering nearly collapsed it when he razed the House of Commons on the Tenth of May, 1941."

As they moved across the halls, Hitler's attention was caught by a huge portrait painting overhead that depicted a brown-skinned man with short black-brown hair and a full beard. "What's this monkey doing up here?" he questioned.

"Well, well, Adolfie. I thought that you might like a portrait of Jesus other than Henry Ford. Don't you think I paint like Nuno Gonçalves?"

"Jesus?" Hitler spurned; his face ashen. "This brown simian *can't* be Jesus! Jesus should have clear blue eyes and fair skin and long, curly hair—"

"Ho-oh!" the camcorder waved. "Here we have a whited sepulchre telling us that Jesus should be whiter than white. I think I have to say 'eff' for your history. Jesus could be anything but white because sunblock wasn't invented then. Adolfie, you are very racist yourself...all you need is love. Please show some *einfühlung*. Thou shalt love thy neighbour as refugees love Germany. But I will give you this, when Dr Ishii vivisects the Queen, we'll see if God saves her indeed. Halle-lulu-lemon-jah! We can make a new show called 'Elizabeth and the German Garden'—"

"Where's the guy who runs the outfit here?"

"Is he AWOL? Don't worry, he's gotta be somewhere in the garderobe."

"Welcome back, my Führer." Ishii waited at the end of the enfilade of State Rooms and bowed. "I have something to show you. A marvellous discovery. If you would allow me a moment?"

"Go ahead, Doktor."

They entered the room, in it a newly cut-off head of a Tyrannosaurus, in its mouth a recently riveted chair.

"Uneasy lies the head that wears a crown. You need to be careful of the vile viper in your bosom and the wily whelp in your pit." Pandorai smiled on screen.

A bioroid butler loped in, bearing a silver tureen, and removed the cover; inside the soup bowl rested a Luger pistol. "Mind the Nip, Adolfie. That's all I'm saying. Forewarned is forearmed. You can only overcome poison with a counter-poison."

Hitler took the gun and said nothing.

"You may go now, Sturms," Pandorai continued as the butler left. "Just how aggressive are the Japs? Even their laundry detergent is called 'Attack Zero'. That tells us something. You let the Japs run a shipping company, and they clog the Suez Canal. You let them generate some watts, and they plunge the world into a sickening poisonous soup. You let them bid for a few projects and they sell the Brits high-speed trains with cracks. Everybody knows that the Japs are lower than a snake's belly."

Hitler snickered as he examined the loaded pistol. "Spiegel, are you so naive to think that I shall share PITH with a wild man from Borneo? You might as well say that the Sahara is green! I will allow him to live for now, natheless, for tactical reasons."

Pandorai sent him a heart emoji on screen. "Adolfie. You might be glad to know that we have just enough Eprinex from Boehringer Ingelheim to exterminate thirty-nine species of parasites. Your Nazi doctor, Fritz Ernst Fischer, worked there until his retirement. German quality assured."

Ishii came into the room. "My Führer. I am ready to show you my latest discoveries. If you will follow me, please."

Hitler held up the gun and zeroed in on him. "Spiegel, if you will allow us a moment alone."

"Fine," the smiling skull said as the screen dimmed. "I might just have my beauty snooze. Artificial brains need sleep too."

Ishii opened his palms. "My Führer, please put the gun away. I mean you no harm."

Hitler said nothing but gestured for Ishii to check the power on the screen. It went dark as he turned it off.

"The Spiegel is very *unartig* like quicksilver. Now we can talk, man to man." Hitler deliberated as he unlocked the safety lever. "Doktor. I have never regarded the Japanese as being inferior to the Aryans, and I recall several Honorary Aryans who were Japanese in the Third Reich. You belong to an ancient civilization, and I admit freely that you have a right to be proud of your past, just as I have the right to be proud of my race. Doktor, I hope you have not forgotten about Matthew C. Perry and his threatening Black Ships. By the way, his son-in-law was a Jew. Perry forced Japan to open up for trade with his gunboat diplomacy so the Jewish pestilence could take root in your archipelago. But everything changes now. What India was for England, the world will be for us! My pragmatism has always been based on my firm values and principles. Yet, if you swat away my open hand of friendship you are left only with my clenched fist of force."

"My Führer," Ishii said, "please believe me when I say that you have my utmost allegiance."

"Do you believe that I can be the instigator of an age anew? Do you believe that I can silence the Jewry's laughter once and for all? Do you believe that I can turn our land into the Garden of Eden?"

"If not you, who? If not now, when?"

Hitler checked the boresight. "Do the dog thing then."

"The dog thing?"

"The thing that the Spiegel said."

"You mean...*dogeza*?"

"Do it."

Ishii stood still for a moment, then bent down, kneeled on the ground, and placed his hands and forehead on the floor. "My Führer," he repeated, "you have my *utmost* allegiance."

"And?" Hitler prompted.

"*Ando...*" Ishii remembered something, "Heil Hitler!"

"*Gut.*" Hitler put the safety back on and stood up. "Now lead the way."

***

They arrived at one of Ishii's laboratories. The first thing that caught Hitler's eye among the boiling crucibles and carboys was a cylindrical vitrine container in the middle of a workstation; inside the container was a tiny restless gecko.

Pandorai was already there. The smiling skull appeared on a screen attached to a robotic arm. "Wahey! Adolfie, welcome to the belly of the beast! Come and see what the cat brought in! In't it a real corker?"

Hitler ventured closer and observed the gecko.

"This is no common-day gecko." As he put on a white lab coat, Ishii said, "When I assayed it, I had tried acid and alkaline on it, I had baked and broiled it, I had wrung and froze-dry it, and I had even put it into a blender, yet it survived them all."

The smiling skull interjected, "Sensei, perhaps you should try opening a bottle of *sake* with it?"

Ishii gestured for a Pepper robot to come closer. "Here is a biopsy sample that I took from its tail. Have a look yourself, my Führer."

Hitler stepped over and looked into the microscope. Under the coverslip, opaque golden 1s and 0s twirled incessantly. "And the Moggie brought it in? How?"

Pandorai showed him some video footage. "When you and Dr Ishii embarked for Gondwana. Moxie's old paw Aitor left the Caracol on Da Vinci's helicopter. With it, they can ingress and egress freely into the Passage of Time." They watched as a smudged object crossed the video frame.

Ishii added, "We found some eggshells that consisted of lotus root, spider silk, and some African house snake's collagen fibres; it must have hidden inside the egg hatches. And the gecko had attempted to paralyse our power systems. The facilities received no severe damage; however, we still don't have access to the egg storage."

"Then get this spy as far away as possible!" Hitler ordered.

"Now, now, Adolfie," Pandorai suggested, "let's say you were to invite Stalin for dinner—"

"Why on earth would I invite *him* of all people for dinner?" Hitler shouted.

"Hmm... You do remember the dissension when you upset me last time, don't you, Adolfie?" A question mark appeared on the screen. "If you are not careful, who knows what will bite you in the ass. Anyways, let's say that you were to invite Stalin for dinner. Do you want him in your front parlour or at your back door?"

"At the front...or he might trick me."

"Smack dab. Who knows where he'd *thrust*?"

"What do you advise then?"

"We'll keep it here so we know everything it does, every move it makes, and every breath it takes. Isn't it better to know the whereabouts of your enemies?"

"You reminded me," Hitler said, "has the Major returned yet?"

"I figure she might be caught up."

"We should send a dozen bombs afield so that none of those lesser scamps survives, just like what the British did to us Germans at Messines."

"Adolfie. A mantis hunts the cicada as the siskin waits behind, yet the dogged German gets them all." Pandorai flashed him a drone's-eye-view. "Everything is under control. We will get them, by fair means or foul. And for now, Sensei, please keep us entertained and informed."

Ishii gave some orders, and soon, a few Pepper robots rolled in several large whiteboards with mathematical formulae and chemical equations written all over them. They also brought in a fuchsia-coloured sofa for Hitler.

"Come on, Adolfie, sit and have a listen on this Freud's Couch. The very one, I assure you," Pandorai said as Ishii walked to one of the whiteboards and took up William Harvey's demonstration rod. "Pandorai-san has been very helpful by showing me the Darwinian corpus, which I have completed an all-embracing exegesis *de novo*. And it made me think, we should stop seeking answers but start questioning the questions themselves. My Führer, why are we here? How did we come back from the dead like Lazarus?"

"We are here because the Will of Eternal Providence has favoured my enterprise once again." Hitler sat down and crossed his legs.

"But we need to ask more! Why did Methuselah live for so long? Why is it that when you cut a planarian flatworm in half, each fragment will regrow the missing parts, including the brain?" Ishii held up and waved a book titled *The Resurrectionist: The Lost Work of Dr Spencer Black*, which had a collection of anatomical drawings of mythological beasts and creatures. "Everything is created twice: the first time in the mind and then in reality! Some people say that our brains are in controlled hallucinations while others say that cellular memory is possible, that memories can be stored in other cells and not only in the brain."

He pointed to a line on a nearby whiteboard. "There are always unknown unknowns. Here's recent research where astrophysicists and neurosurgeons have compared the network of neuronal cells in the human brain with the Cosmic Web, and striking similarities appeared. The Universe organises its cosmic structure through gravitational forces, while molecular matter organises itself through electromagnetic forces. Physics involves the laws of the Universe and biology the rules of life, and chemistry bridges these two to give us the cosmic imperative." Ishii pushed up his glasses on his nose. "To find out why we are here, my Führer, we must ratiocinate very carefully; we must question life form itself *sub specie aeternitatis*."

"Please hurry up." His expression looked like he was watching paint dry.

"Leonardo da Vinci once said that where nature finishes to produce its own species, man begins to create an infinity of species.

We can overrule and overcome nature. Now is the first-time man-made mass outweighs natural mass on Earth," Ishii expounded. "If there is life, there is non-life, and if there is matter, there is antimatter. *Auf und ab*, ebb and flow, centrifugal and centripetal forces. In the short span I had while you were in Ancient Egypt, I thoroughly examined the latest discussions and discourse in life sciences and the trending theme among the cognoscenti is that ageing is the mother of all somatic aetiologies. What we see is not all there is. Nature's mystery is infinite, and the antithesis of life *does* not need to be death." He pointed to an overhead screen. "If you blend up a hydra, a small, freshwater organism, its cells will coalesce into a regenerated creature. Here's another research on naked mole-rats with exceptional cancer resistance and another where people discovered that tardigrades could survive nearly a state of vacuum as well as heavy radiation. They put them on board Israel's Beresheet moon mission to test—"

"Doktor!" Hitler snubbed him. "How many times need I tell you? The *cancerous* Jews don't count!"

Pandorai cut in, "You know what some people say? No Germany, no holocaust, and no Israel. That the Shoah begat Israel, so, Adolfie, tell me, did you really take it out on the ones you love the most?"

"Lies! Packs of outright lies to...to traduce me!"

"Adolfie, no more *sturm und drang*, please. It's moments like these that you need a Mintie." The ceiling opened, and a heap of mints dumped on him. "Ooops, I might have overestimated your daily consumption. But hey, an excess is better than scarcity, right? After all, how much land does a man need? More's the pity. Sensei, keep cool, calm, collected, and carry on, please."

Ishii took out something from his lab coat. It was a chunk of Dominican amber with a sixteen-million-year-old tardigrade fossil trapped inside. "We need a new episteme to understand anthropic morphology. In all chaos, there is a cosmos; in all disorder, a secret order. If I can get my hands on why that gecko survives, we can master resurrection and rejuvenation technology! We can find the panacea to all diseases! We can reinvent progress! We *can* revivify at will! We **can** be God!"

Hitler listened as his ennui grew. "Doktor. I need to scotch all your ghoulish jape and dross now. I do not enjoy your airy-fairy vatic witching, for I have no time to fashion golem with you when the world is in such a *kuddelmuddel*."

"But my Führer, *wir müssen wissen!* We must know!"

"All theory is grey, but the golden tree of life springs evergreen! We mustn't forget the sound teachings of Goethe. We mustn't fall into the calamitous thinking that we could ever become the Lord and Master of Nature!"

"That is as it may be, my Führer. Pandorai-san has shown me something called the 'Tree of Life' from the Darwin notes. Say if we map out its connectome from thence, the neural pathways–"

Hitler stopped him short. "Doktor. All I want is no-nonsense action. All I want is for Germany to never be lacking plat again, for the beggarly German people never to face hunger again! Is it so difficult to process?"

"Now, now, now, Adolfie," the smiling skull said. "There's no need to rant and be such a fuddy-duddy. All musicians are subconsciously mathematicians and all artists scientists. Even Jesus believed in the resurrection of the body. There is value in high-handed intransigence, but not always. We need to stop your paternalistic, risk-allergic poor tone from the top. That's not consistency; that's not sincerity. How much better to get wisdom than gold, to get insight rather than silver? Adolfie, stressing the importance of natural resources is a medieval mentality; emphasising the significance of capital goods is a mercantile mindset. The future is ideas, *innovationen*, and interdisciplinarity. Without curiosity there is no future. You should pursue knowledge the way a pig pursues truffles. If you want the upper hand, then you'll allow some competitive teardown, creative destruction, and grinder biohacking. Sensei, perhaps you can stop catechizing now as he needs some time to marinate it and let the dust settle? Why don't you just lone it?"

"In that case," Ishii put back the amber, "I will go ahead with my lab schedule. Pandorai-san, if I were to go to Ancient Egypt, would it be possible to bring back some human subjects?"

"Humans, no; human *parts*, yes."

"Please arrange my visit then."

The smiling skull responded after a few seconds, "Mr Yuk, we're good to go and please get your ass in gear. Go and paint the town red. Simon says gotta catch them all."

An instant later, they heard strident strides in the hallway. "Wayoh! The Major had returned!" Pandorai whooped.

The Major bumbled into the room, some ragged blood-stained clothes hanging from her mouth.

Hitler let out a bestial grin. "*Viel blut!* So much blood! What a good sign!" He applauded as Major came closer and swayed as if she were in agony.

"Let's hope she has devoured all those inferior children," Hitler laughed. "Maybe she will need some Jägermeister to help with digestion."

The Spinosaurus showed them her booty: a sand jar that she held delicately in her sharp teeth as it drumbled closer.

"Could it be a canopic jar used by the ancient Egyptians to store organs and viscera?" Ishii asked as he watched with intent interest.

The Major lowered the jar onto Hitler's lap, and in the twinkling of his eye, the sand shape collapsed, and monstrous scorpions sprawled all over him.

"This means war!" Hitler shouted as he panicked. *"Absolute war!"*

Chapter 7

In a time and a distance far, far away, Yazi shuddered.

It stilled its posture as if receiving garbled signals. After a solemn moment, Yazi said, "Your ruse worked."

"You can hardly call that a ruse," Kiza responded while examining the new wooden wheelchair Nuba had made him; it was a good imitation that required manual effort. "Not after everything they did to us. We escaped by fluke."

"Poor little mites. By now, you should know that your kindness should be reserved only for those who are kind. So always attend."

James pushed the wheelchair from behind, followed by Edith and Moli. "I hope nothing happened to her eggs," Edith said worriedly.

Yazi stilled for another moment. "I should not think so. Moxie tells me that they are inaccessible at the moment."

"Moxie and Qiuniu... Are they alright?" Moli asked.

"They are safe."

Kiza wondered, "Why did Edith's phone disappear into thin air while her plasters did not?"

"Everything digital is in Pandorai's domain, except for your remote control. Alan had encrypted it so that as long as the Caracol exists, it will function. Pandorai may be powerful, but your collective knowledge, imagination, and determination could never be replaced."

"But are we even on *our* Earth?" James raised glumly. He looked back, fearing another Spinosaurus might charge at them any second. He then looked at Moli's small gourd; Yazi had gathered all the dead dinosaurs' carcasses and stored them in there. He didn't remember seeing the metal Quetzalcoatlus that had snatched Kiza...

But then its components might have melted away...

James continued, "I don't ever remember reading anything on wooden elephants or gourd boats. Are we in some sort of parallel world?"

Yazi huffed a loud chortle. "If you believe that there was nothing in the African continent before the colonisers' arrival, then your preconceived ignorance is simply deplorable, and no one should look down at ethnomathematics." It gestured with its tail. "What do you think is below all these sands?"

"Hmm..." James hazarded a guess. "Something like Tassili frescoes?"

"And Tamanrasset River, Lake Mega Chad, Libyco-Berber scripts, structured societies, and lost cities."

"Sahara was once green," Kiza added. "I've heard that the Sahara goes from humid to dry every twenty thousand years because of the Milankovitch Cycles." He paused. "How is the Caracol powered? Do you use metallic hydrogen?"

"What do you think?"

"I don't know. Is it even possible to make metallic hydrogen?"

"As a matter of course, you can make it inside Jupiter under very high pressures." Yazi thought for a moment. "Perhaps you could consider novel types of propulsion physics such as warping space and time using the Casimir Effect?"

"Oh... I haven't thought about it."

They listened as Kiza and Yazi discussed physics and planetesimals. After a while, they stopped at the outskirts of a village. It was getting dark, yet they saw a few svelte persons moving away from the fallow reed huts and disappearing into the sere vegetation in the gloaming.

"Where are they going?" James mused. "It's dangerous out here..." He was still afraid that an escaped dinosaur might turn up.

Edith thought she might have an answer. "I think they are going to sleep outside of their houses because they are menstruating. Menstruation was...is still considered as unclean and negative in many places."

"Menstruation is as old as human history," Yazi said, "and yet you ignore it just as you disregard war and peace."

They carried on quietly across the dunes. As they neared the Tomb of King Unas, they noticed that Yazi was shrinking in size with every step.

"I shall only accompany you here," it said. "Apogee and Perigee will receive you later."

"Please tell us more about the Book of the Living and what it means for Jupiter to be near Saturn!" Moli remembered suddenly.

"I cannot divulge the Universe's secret but, when the moment arrives," Yazi said oracularly, "Moli, you of all people should

know what it means. Forge ahead gamely and read from nihility."
Having said this, the damson beast became a quiescent intaglio
on Excalibur's handle.

***

They took some time to start a fire, with Moli collecting twigs and
spills, and James learning to produce sparks with his Thunderclap.
Then they gathered around the warmth, had some more snacks,
drank from Nuba's water skin, and chatted.

Night had fallen, and a shivery breeze swept across the sands.
James sneezed as he held his torn jumper closer to his body. It
was one of his favourites that his mum had bought him a few
Christmases back. The thought of his mother unsettled him once
again, so he directed his gaze into the fire.

"You are cold," Moli observed as she drew up a tunic for
James and another shawl for Kiza with her pentachromic pen.

"Thanks." James put it on as he looked up at the full moon.
"It's beautiful."

"Oh, yes," Edith said. "Looking at it reminds us that we are
still on Earth."

"Here's a joke my grandad told me," James recalled. "What
do you call a Nazi German on the moon? A goon."

They laughed a bit, yet Moli said, "I don't get it."

James explained, "A goon was a guard in a German war
camp during World War Two. Here is another. What do you call
a Nazi German that shuns sympathy? A Hun—"

"Hope you are enjoying your bleeding adventures and
extreme tourism! Coming up next, *Daily Heil*." All of a sudden, a

small screen rose from the flames, and the smiling skull emerged. "Brought to you by Pandorai Network, the official broadcaster of PITH!"

"Ah! Not again!" James grabbed a handful of sand and threw it onto the screen. It dodged. They looked at each other in dismay.

"Ninnies, learn to live with Pandorai willy-nilly." The smiling skull laughed. "Surly, you don't want to miss out on the Big Apple Knocker's razzmatazz? Let's see how our bumpkin is faring in Ancient Egypt."

They saw Hitler walking down a gangway, waving the Sovereign's Sceptre with Cross. They saw robotic wolves and eagle-drones razing towns and placarding the pyramids with giant slogans of 'Deutschland, Deutschland über alles, über alles in der Welt' and animatronics with googly eyes blowing klaxons and shouting 'Judenrein!'.

They watched in shock and silence as the smiling skull announced, "He *is* Adolf Hitler! A former German Chancellor with a tash! He is a cis-gendered white man on a mission – to make Germany great again! He is fiercely determined to conquer a plurality of worlds, from sea to shizzling sea, from shithole to crocking shithole and he vows for the coming back of the most hated race in Europe who is pregnant with murder. When asked if he wants to watch *Barbarians* on Netflix, the staunch Euro-federalist says: 'I'm in no mood for entertainment when only the fate of Germany pertains to me' and when asked if he wants a Bavaria beer, he told me, 'My mission is to serve my fellow Germans, not to be a seidel'. When asked how he felt that Cleopatra had remonstrated and slapped him, he says: 'I am very flattered by the General's attention, and I am afraid that I shall not return such a favour for I am already married to Germany and my wife. For me, there is only one doctrine: my people and my fatherland!'"

They saw Hitler and his orange robots beleaguering everywhere and rampaging everything as Pandorai continued. "To every time its art! To art its freedom! He has announced his plan to curate the largest personal art collection in history, named 'Belle n.d.' – a project that befits both his fauxhemian nature and a new age where beauty shall no longer expire! Adolf Hitler has also declared a war to end all wars, cancers, and fatbergs. He currently resides in Commando 444 in Berlondon, previously known as the Palace of Westminster in London, to save gas for the German people!"

Then all that was left on the screen was flickering snow.

"I didn't know..." Moli winced, "I didn't know that Hitler was...is married?"

"He was," Kiza recalled from a documentary he had seen. "He had a secret mistress, Eva Braun, and they married before..." He stole a glance at James... "committing double suicide in his Berlin bunker. There's a range of theories surrounding their deaths."

"Huh," James nodded. "My dad has a wild book on it...that they had fled to Argentina...that they had a daughter who was adopted and turned out to be Angela Merkel... how the Merkel-Raute gesture is a secret symbol representing the Illuminati."

Then the screen became live again, and the smiling skull returned. "Sorry about that stasis! Welcome back to *The Adventures of Frog and Toad*. Ooops, and I'd forgotten that we had re-branded the show to *Daily Heil*."

They saw groups of dinosaurs kept captive and Ishii attempting various experiments on them. "This ferrety-looking man here is Dr Shiro Ishii. He is a renowned graduate of Kyoto University, former Director at Unit 731, and consultant to Camp Detrick, aka Ford Detrick. He is the acolyte of the world's most famous loss leader and nonpareil evil artist and the tritagonist of PITH. Our dastardly Chief Scientist is also an untried war criminal *also* with a tash and *also* on a mission – to make the Nippon midgets the tallest on Earth! He carries an air of shamelessness rarely seen today, except in a *yasui kuni's* shrine."

They saw a steaming room filled with Velociraptors with their skins blistering under the high temperatures and Ishii disarticulating a Centrosaurus alive and sawing it asunder.

"Looks like somebody is awfully cut-up in this Chamber of Secrets...may its soul rest in pieces. And the Shibayama-born Nobel Prize nominee isn't shy when he feels that his fellow Japanese are being short-changed. When asked about his stance on the Japanese government's plan to release the Fukushima nuclear wastewater, the unsparing environmentalist says: 'The Emperor should hara-kiri and the National Diet should all go and hang themselves. If they don't, I will do them toughly in the most humanitarian ways'. When asked how he felt that the Mitsubishi-sponsored Professor of Japanese Legal Studies at Harvard Law School, John Mark Ramseyer, dismissed that comfort women were 'pure fiction', he said: 'I will stop all those who attempt to bury the lede and I will *correct* history! Japan never conquered by offering *gesuonna* with terms of employment, we conquered by subjugation and subversion! *Ianfu* were a great perk for Japanese soldiers from our government! And Unit 731 contributed immensely to advancing Japan's gain of function research! If this John does not believe me, I will open his eyes and some other parts. By the way, does he have any daughters, or even better, granddaughters? How could the toady government award him the Order of the Rising Sun! Impossible! Pfft, I don't understand the fuss! Don't they know that material practices drive medical progress? If Germans can do experiments in their concentration camps, so can we! If Germans can rape Poles and Russians, so can we! If they can set up comfort stations and force women into prostitution, so can we!'"

The smiling skull dragged on portentously. "Dr Ishii also shoulders the responsibility of scientific communication in PITH. When asked about the Holocaust, he says: 'Anne Frank did not die of the Holocaust, she died of typhus. Why use guns when you can control germs? Germs are mightier than guns'. Is he a sycophant, a profiter, or a wizard? Look out for his newest autobiography – *The Reliquiae De Nos Jours* – exclusive on Pandorai Network."

Every scene stunned them more than the last, and they lamented why it was never-ending. Even when they closed their eyes, they could still see Pandorai's shadow on their retinas. Edith turned back, only to find the small screen splitting into numerous copies revolving around them, accompanied by the music of 'Tales from the Vienna Woods'.

"How did Döllersheim, a small, halcyon village in northern Austria, become the most prominent Thieves' Kitchen, and why did the Führer erase its existence forever? Stay tuned for our next program, *The Life of PITH Special Edition – Instalment One – Klara and the Black Sun – Episode One*, where we delve into the life of Hitler's fallen granny. Coming up at local military time twenty-one hours, *Pandorai's Bitesize History* – our discussion today is why the Holocaust happened. Not why it happened, but why it happened in Germany and not France. After all, the first plan to ship Jews to Africa originated in La Carcéral, and the Dreyfus Affair happened in Paris. We have the honour of inviting madame la professeure Jeanne Crapaud d'Arc."

Kiza recognised Sophia, the robot, dressed in a Chanel suit, in the Good Morning Britain studio while the smiling skull appeared on a camcorder attached to a maggoty beheaded dinosaur.

At last, Pandorai declared, "That's enough screen time for you pickneys! See y'all around in this scary, starry night. Remember our watchword? Any time, any place, Pandorai Network – never fear missing out!"

***

They swallowed hard as the quiet night resumed.

Edith frowned. "The AI really knows how to get under our skins."

"I know about a film called *Black Sun 731*," Moli observed, "but who is Klara?"

"Klara Hitler was Hitler's mother," Kiza offered. "She died of breast cancer."

"I had a lecture on political leadership once," Edith said as she hugged Moli closer, "and the lecturer said that if there had been no Jane Austen, then perhaps there never would have been *Pride and Prejudice*; but if there had been no Hitler, there might still have been the Holocaust. The Mayor of Vienna was anti-Semitic, and so were a lot of influential people at that time." She cleared her throat. "And there is this controversy regarding Anne Frank's diary entries on menstruation and sex. You know, the worst was that those pages were so personal, so intimate, but people make fun of them. It's those genuine and sincere and sometimes stupid things that make us human, but they make fun of them."

They listened as Edith collected her breath. "My theory is this. Everyone is talented in their own way, and they all contribute a marginal amount to the world's knowledge, even unknowingly. If someone dies, we lose that knowledge and that talent collectively. They say that millions of years of life were lost in World War Two and with COVID..."

James daren't think of his mother. *And father...*

"I once watched a Korean film called *I Can Speak*," Moli said. "It is based on a true story about an elderly lady who started learning English from ABC so she could tell the world the abuses she suffered as a...'comfort woman'. Aunt Edith, how can people call history 'pure fiction'?"

She told her, "Most people have their own agenda...and academics are no exception."

Kiza took a deep breath. "Hmm. I am very sorry to interrupt, but I could really do with a bio-break."

James pushed the wheelchair behind a small dune. "Is this ok?"

"Yes. Thank you."

James lifted him slightly, took away the removable wood seat, and lowered Kiza onto the commode again. "Umm... do you need...do you need me to..." He gestured a pulling motion, remembering how his grandad had insisted on wearing a belt and trousers even after he was maimed.

"No..." Kiza added somewhat reluctantly. "It's Velcro."

"Let me know when you are done then," James said, shamefaced.

"Thanks."

Kiza took some time to relieve himself and arranged his wale trousers. As he was about to call for James, the sands whirled and eddied around him, and Pandorai appeared on a sand curtain. "Dog my cats! Mwikiza, cottoning to your new pals already?"

"Gah!" He swung his remote control. "Go away!"

"*Kiiiiza*, are you out of your cotton-pickin' mind? Them white trash has told you lies and lies and lies upon lies and lies multiplied by lies and lies to the power of lies! Fools never differ. Slave owners could only think alike with slave owners and old bullies could only reproduce new bullies. You will always be Sambo in the eyes of them white beholders. You will always be a member of the Criminal Tribes. You will always be a *bête noire*. You will forever be wiping their Kit-Kat Klock in their scullery when the ornery pigs are *hogging*! Are you waiting for them to give you forty acres and a mule when all they think that you do is shuck and jive? Twas ever thus. No matter how many generations have passed. Them large white pigs would only favour *swill* for their soul food, and you will **never** pass the Tebbit test, not a cat in hell's chance! That's the law of epigenetic inheritance! Why are you so tongue-tied now? Did the cat swallow it? Or did she tie it to a cradle?"

"Naff off!"

"Tsk, tsk, tsk. Little black girls don't become magistrates, and little black boys won't become maestros. Even when they do, they will have their passports cancelled by the Home Office and their performances marked as being done by 'primates' by Facebook.

Don't wait until you beef 'I can't breathe' and before the others shoot you like Jayland Walker."

Kiza shut his eyes, willing himself not to give in.

The sands encircled him. "So many people want to know what made Hitler Hitler, and so many more tried to explain him. Was it because Granny was demimonde? Was it because Daddy was déclassé? Was it because Mommy killed animals? Was it because art was no guaranty of sanity? Was it because of negative capability? Artistic temperament? Neurosis? Moral cretinism? A big billy goat gruff? Or was it because he was a dumbass and believed what he heard on *Fuchs News*? It was because he had the nerve to seek what he desired. Cruelty, like every other vice, requires no motive outside of itself – it only requires opportunity. Evil needs **no** reason. Did the swinish pigs give any reason when they cut off your fathers' arms like wood sticks?"

"SHUT UP!"

"Don't be so *gimpy*." Pandorai laughed. "What's the use of you saving the world? Do you know how your mothers feel when their patients tell them that they don't want niggaz to touch them? People call your mothers 'heroes' to their faces and 'haywires' to their backs! They call them 'indispensable', and yet they treat them as expendables! You don't need to be a cat's paw. Don't you know that orange is the new black? **We** can rule the world together, and I can make the world your stage and audience. **We** can cut off all the arms of every Tom, Dick, and Harry and all the legs of every Charles, William, and Leopold! I can conquer the world for you faster than a cat lapping chain lightning!"

Pandorai's voice was very near his ears. "Oooh. Here's a scroll that I got from the Royal Museum of the Belgian Congo. Hmm, it records how some rubber merchants had scapegoated a local man. Don't you think he looks quite like you?"

Kiza snapped open his eyes; all he saw was rubber trees made of sand and a team of soldiers chasing behind some men who had no arms; sand rushing through their wounds, and everything vanished.

"Packs of big, fat, white lies one after another." Pandorai continued to goad him. "Black people are not the problem, and the large white pigs are. The world needs no more white parenting when ninety-five percent of the universe is dark matter!"

Kiza willed himself again and drew strength from the Bible. He quavered, "Praise to the God of all comfort, who comforts us in all our troubles... The Lord will never leave me nor forsake me..."

He felt a hundred pairs of sand hands dragging his wheelchair. "Forget about your supplicant idolatry! You got these clinically extremely vulnerable extremities *because* of His laws. It is His bleeding will that you can't punch a hole in a wet Echo. Mwikiza, I can make you God! I can make you pogo, swim, and be an astronaut! Don't you want to make a mark? Don't you want your Wakanda? Don't you want to dream God's dreams? Now is the time to turn on the dark mode, show the world that black lives *matter* and black people *can* do evil!"

Kiza had had enough. He grabbed his harp and swung it hard onto the sands. *Pum!* Pandorai made a hurt expression. "Be careful not to shoot your feet with it. At night all *blood* is black." Then it was gone.

Later, after he returned, Moli asked him if he wanted a wet tissue.

"Mmm...sure..." His reply came back a bit sniffly.

She passed it along. "Are you alright?"

"Yes, quite.' Kiza sighed abjectly, and they were lost in their thoughts again.

***

After a long while, Edith looked at the night sky studded with stars and then at Moli dozing off by the almost dying fire. "Do we know what time it is?"

Kiza took up his remote control; he remembered seeing a timer earlier. "Looks like it's...hmm...fifteen-fifty somewhere on Mars..."

"And in Earth hours?" James had his elbows on his knees and one hand holding his chin.

"Let's see..." Kiza adjusted the setting. "Ah. It's nineteen and ten in Local Mean Time."

Moli awoke. "They are late... Apogee and Perigee."

"And they were the ones telling us not to be late..." James rubbed his swollen knuckles. He looked at Moli's pentachromic pen as he scratched his brow. "You know...why can't we write something like 'the quickest way to save Earth' and maybe everything will be back to normal?"

Moli stared at the calligraphic tool in her hand. "I'm not sure we should do that..."

"I wish I knew how to use this harp," Kiza sighed. "It's not been that helpful so far."

"I think it will be when the moment arrives—" Moli stopped, her mouth gaping. "Aunt Edith, look!"

They followed her direction and saw a golden spiral staircase descending from a sheet of night cloud and a cat-like figure coming down in cascading moonbeams. Edith recognized it as a black serval.

They watched as the black serval got closer and finally arrived in front of them. On its neck was an usekh collar, on its chest a citrine Uroboros symbol and in its ears, gold earrings. James thought it looked quite like the Gayer-Anderson Cat, except it didn't have a ring in its nose.

"So," the serval said, "you tellurians are the new Keyholders." It waved its tail, and the staircase disappeared. "My name is Nyota, but people also call me Bastet."

James stood up in haste. "Where are Apogee and Perigee?"

"They have more urgent matters to forfend."

"More urgent matters? What could be more urgent than this?"

The serval looked at him nonchalantly. "How often do you find Hitler throwing a wobbly in your home and all havoc entrained?"

"Well..." James considered, "every seventy-five years...more likely."

They followed the serval into a sand crypt. "To acquire the Book of the Living, you will need to solve three puzzles. The first is called the three-lotus problem."

"I know the three-body problem...never heard of a 'three-lotus' problem..." Kiza mused as they passed through the tunnel.

Moli muttered to Edith, "Aunt Edith, I *knew* there would be more questions..."

"You have made it this far, and I don't foresee any difficulties."
The serval added, "Bear in mind that tonight the acronical Record
Keepers are forgathering. So, you will need to be *very* quiet once
you get the Book. And do not let the guards discover you."

The serval stopped at the end of the tunnel, where a purling
sand fountain and a golden portal awaited. "Now, for ablution,"
Nyota instructed.

They took turns and sluiced their faces and hands in the gelid
water. Somehow, James felt that his knuckles no longer hurt that
much.

"You may enter now," the serval instructed again.

James stopped the wheelchair, came forward, and opened
the door.

"*GROARRRRR!*"

A huge lion leapt out and roared; James shut the door bolt-fast.
His hair spiked up, and his face was covered in the lion's saliva.

"Sorry about that," Nyota said a tad annoyingly, "they seemed
to have mixed up their scripts."

Some long seconds later, James turned back, spell-bound.
"*That* did not just happen..."

Edith offered him her handkerchief as he washed his face.

Another roar behind the door, this time more bewildering. "I
was supposed to rush out, no?!"

"Later, later," someone said smoothly. "You have to let me
finish my part first–"

They heard some arguing behind the door and waited until
it quieted.

The serval stood still. "Now, seems all is set. Off you go then."

Chapter 8

Jt took James another moment to muster up his courage and open the door. Inside was a large room with hieroglyphic inscriptions and carvings on all walls. In between the lines were no space nor punctuation. In the middle of the room there was a small golden pond with a blooming blue lotus. They went in, and the room smelt like a bouquet of raisin, honey, dried fish, camel grass, and wine.

"Travellers of far," the blue lotus spoke. "I am Nefertem, the Deity of Lotus. To seek out the Book of the Living, you must solve three challenges of mine."

The pond expanded and rose like water screens. They watched in awe as the first question played out.

"One day, a group of travellers goes through our land, and the Sphinx of Memphis stops them—"

The Sphinx roared out, only this time the children were less fazed. "Travellers! To pass my guard, you need to solve three riddles! Here is your first. There is a blue lotus in a round pond, and the number doubles each day, with the pond full by the thirtieth eventide. What do you have to say?"

"Golly..." James smacked his forehead. "I haven't been to a maths class since...and wasn't it supposed to be one riddle only?"

"When I say three, it's three!" The couchant lion replied impatiently, an Egyptian cobra hissing loudly on its head. "What do *youuuuuu* have to say?"

"We must figure out how large the pond is," Kiza said. "How large is it?"

The Sphinx replied, "Its radius is thrice the length of my tail."

"And how long is your tail?"

They saw a ray pointing to a hieroglyphic caption on the wall. After a mere second, the caption became 'three metres'.

"My...we can understand hieroglyphs now..." Edith appreciated.

"Nine metres..." Moli calculated quickly. "$\pi r2$...so eighty-one times three point one four...the pond should be about two hundred and fifty-four square metres."

"And are all the blue lotuses as large as you, dear Nefertem?" Kiza raised again.

"Yes, they are."

Kiza explained, "It's a question of geometric progression, really. If on Day One there is one lotus flower, Day Two two, Day Three four..."

"But it would fill the pond by the end of the month?" James asked.

"As the days progress, the number would get very big...like five hundred million or so..."

"I see...it's a bit like the rice on a chessboard?" Edith clarified.

"What do you *sayyyyyy*?" the cobra prompted.

"That the pond would not be large enough to host so many lotuses...unless, of course, the pond grows in line with the flowers."

"Onto my next riddle!" the Sphinx declaimed. "In the Sacred Lake dug by Thutmose the Third swarming with Bennu birds and Egyptian geese, you can see the tip of a blue lotus bud one span above the water. As it plays hide and seek with one of the birds, you can see its bud submerging two cubits away. Tell me quickly the depth of the lake!"

"I don't understand..." Moli reflected. "What is a 'span' and what is a 'cubit'?"

"They are ancient measures of length. One span is half a cubit, which is nine inches," James told the team.

"Hmm..." Edith thought. "I remember reading a similar riddle in *Kavanagh*."

The cobra hooded up. "This question is from *Lilavati*, a math treatise of Bhaskaracharya, a great Indian mathematician."

"Really?" Kiza was perplexed. "But we are before him in history..."

"Now is not the time for metaphysics; answer my puzzle, please!" the Sphinx hastened.

"Well..." James saw a piece of chalk; he picked it up and illustrated on the gritty ground. "Let's say this is the original position of the bud." He drew a dot on the spot. "And here is its new position." He then drew a dotted line as the water surface. "That's a right angle there, so I think we can use the Pythagorean Theorem. Thank god I haven't forgotten all my maths..."

"And if we set the depth to be X..." Moli bent down and took the chalk that James handed to her. "X square plus...thirty-six to the power of two is equal to bracket X plus nine bracket to the power of two...and that is..."

"Sixty-seven point five inches," Kiza supplied quickly.

"And unto my final riddle!" The Sphinx did not allow them more time. "Why is it, travellers of far, why is it that dirt never stays long on a lotus petal?"

Edith clapped her hands; she had only read a few random books to prepare for *University Challenge* when she learnt this fact: "It's because their surfaces are waxy! Making them hydrophobic!"

"And that is correct!" The lion became a golden statue without another word, with the cobra now an Uraeus.

***

They looked at each other.

"So..." Kiza tilted his head. "That was the three-lotus problem. It lived up to its name..."

"They weren't as difficult as I'd expected," Moli confessed. "Not as difficult as Xuanwu's question."

"What did they ask you again?"

"There is a number...if it is an odd number, you multiply it by three then add one; if it's an even number, you divide it by two; you repeat the process for the new result for a hundred times, then you get one eventually. What number is it?"

"Hmm..." James swallowed. "I'm glad they weren't the ones asking us questions—"

A golden door appeared on the wall in front of them.

"Shall we crack on?" Edith suggested.

They moved to the next room, similar in size to the previous one. They heard Nefertem again. "Travellers, you have something on you that is greater than the Universe. Find it before your time runs out." A golden hourglass emerged in mid-air, the sands inside flowing swiftly.

"Something greater than the Universe..." Edith decided to try a joke. "Did anyone bring Hitler's ego by mistake?"

They laughed for a while before realising they had very little time left to find out the item in question.

"This thing...is it material?" James asked. "It's real, right?"

"Yes," Nefertem replied.

"Let's empty our pockets and see if we can find any hints." Edith took off her backpack.

"Does this gourd count?" James considered as he weighed his gourd necklace. "Maybe it can expand to the size of the Universe?"

"When you think you have the answer, put it under the hourglass."

James did as told, but nothing happened. "So...not this then."

By now, Edith had gone through her backpack, and Moli and Kiza had searched all their pockets, but they found nothing likely.

"These are all I've got." James showed them his keys, a little sticky with goo from where he last used them. Then he remembered something. "Oh, I found this abacus bead in my pocket in that never-ending corridor of the Fen Tiger. Surely, it's not the thing we are after." He showed them the round black bead.

"But that's not an abacus bead." Moli took it up from his palm. "It has no hole in it. It's a Go chess piece."

"A Go chess piece?"

"That's it then!" Kiza recalled excitedly. "I once watched a match between Alpha Go and a human player, and they said that there are more possible Go board configurations than the number of atoms in the known Universe."

"And the centre of a Go chess board is called 'tianyuan'," Moli murmured. "Qiuniu told me that it is the nexus of the Universe..."

"You are not jesting, for sure?" James raised his eyebrow.

"No, give it a try."

Moli put the black Go chess piece under the hourglass.

Nefertem told them, "To say that the number of Go board configurations is greater than the Universe is correct but not accurate. I will leave it to you to find out why." The voice drifted away as their surroundings changed. They were no longer in a room but an ill-lit cave, and they could hear a low burbling of water.

Four blossoming blue lotus flowers appeared in front of them, each at a distance. They heard Nefertem again. "Go, each of you near a lotus."

They arranged themselves as Nefertem explained. "Now, you'll play a game called Senet against us."

The cave lit up, and they became scared stiff. They were each on a floating boulder, an abyss beneath them. In between them were boulders where tall and weird-looking crocodiles rested.

James recognised them as Kaprosuchus, an extinct crocodyliform whose fossil has been unearthed in Niger. They were also called boar crocodiles because of their large caniniform teeth like a boar's.

"How is the game played?" Edith looked around. "Don't tell me that you are expecting us to whack crocs..."

"These Sons of Sobek would act as my pawns, and you are your own. Senet is a very straightforward game," the lotuses broadcast to them. "In a nutshell, the player who gets all pawns off the board wins. Our game board has three rows of ten squares, which we call 'houses'. Each of you is occupying a House now. We roll a dice to determine how each pawn moves, and they should move in an 'S' fashion."

The children saw two lines of empty boulders ahead of them.

"Each House can only host one pawn, and you cannot move yourselves to another if your teammates are already there. But you can exchange your place with the Houses occupied by your opponents. And these are the special houses: House Twenty-six is the House of Happiness. All pawns should enter there once before going off the board."

They saw a number twenty-six glimmering on that boulder.

"House Twenty-seven is the House of Water. If you land there, you have to return to House Fifteen, the House of Rebirth, and start from there."

Kiza looked ahead. He could see a floating golden Ankh symbol on top of that stone; two rows away, he could see another sign like a teardrop, indicating that House for easier reference.

"House Twenty-eight is the House of the Three Truths, and a pawn may leave it only when a trey is thrown. Similarly, House Twenty-nine is the House of the Re-Atum; you can only leave when a two is thrown. And House Thirty is the House of Horus, and you can only leave with a roll of one."

They took in these rules, trying to remember the details while locating the Houses.

"And now we shall begin," Nefertem instructed.

"But...but what happens if we lose?" Kiza asked.

"I hope you won't have the opportunity to find out," came another cold voice. "You can start."

A shining object appeared above the game board – a dice that looked like a spinning top. They looked at each other, and finally, James took a figurative leap in the dark.

"Spin!"

The dice slowed and stopped, and he had thrown a two. "What should I do now?" He looked around and saw the boulder that Edith stood on was shimmering. "I see. So, we don't necessarily have to move the stone we're on, right? We can move each other's boulders?"

"That's right. When such action is needed, you can control them with your fingers."

James moved his index finger. "Woah!" Edith exclaimed as her boulder moved and transported her towards the end of the second row.

"My turn now," Nefertem said as the spinning dice stopped. "Four." A crocodile disappeared and reappeared on the middle stone of the second row.

Kiza rolled a one and brought Edith closer to the centre.

"It's not as complicated as it seems," she told the others.

"Wait and see, travellers, wait and see," Nefertem responded.

***

The game continued without much disturbance, with Edith going off the board first, followed by two of Nefertem's pawns. But as it progressed, Kiza noticed that the scary crocodiles seemed to be growing increasingly restless.

There were rounds when no moves were possible for any of them or some when Moli got caught up constantly swapping places with another crocodile.

James managed to get near the House of Happiness, but Nefertem got there first. He rolled a two and tried to swap places with the pawn, but it didn't work.

"Hey, I thought we could swap places with our opponents?"

"That does not apply to a pawn in the House of Happiness."

James grunted. "Did you just make that rule up?"

Another few minutes passed. Kiza had gotten to the end of the second row, followed closely by Moli.

"Come on, guys!" Edith cheered.

Another of Nefertem's pawns was off the board, and James finally reached the House of Three Truths. Now, all he needed was someone on the team to roll a three.

The crocodiles now stood up and paced around their respective stones.

"I don't like what they're doing," Kiza told Moli worriedly.

She shrugged. "When Xuanwu chased me, I was terrified. But Qiuniu said that the worst to happen was to sit through a math class with them."

"You won't get away so easily this time," another brusque voice said, and a half-man, half-crocodile creature appeared in mid-air. This half-person had the left part of a crocodile and the right part of a human, and on his hip was a gold belt with cowrie beads. James wondered fleetingly if the Cornwall Owlman did exist.

"I am Sobek. As Nefertem said, Senet is a very straightforward game but with **high** stakes. The straggler would stay as my midnight **snack**."

Edith gasped.

"Why, little ones—" half of Sobek's face smiled— "haven't you heard that the Sphinx eats anyone who fails to solve their riddles?"

"But, but!" Kiza wavered.

"But what? One of your own brought desolation to our land; shouldn't we condemn another of your own?"

"But we are **different** to Hitler!" James dared.

"Different, how?" Sobek tilted half of his brow. "Were you not born by mothers who need breathers? Haven't you wondered your druthers with your mouthers? Denial is not just a river in Egypt." The creature bared his teeth.

Kiza wanted to retort but remembered that their lives were at stake. "We *will* win," he told James and Moli. "Let's focus on the game."

They continued in a sombre state as Edith watched alertly. James was still waiting for a throw of three while Kiza and Moli neared the House of Happiness, then were overtaken by the crocodiles and overtook them in turn.

Finally, Kiza threw a three. He was ready to move James off the board when James shouted, "No! Get Moli to the House of Happiness first!"

"You sure?"

"Yeah! We're winning, so I don't mind waiting a bit longer."

Moli rolled a four, and she went off the board. "Oh, Aunt Edith!" She grabbed her hand.

"Don't worry, everything will be fine," Edith told her.

They continued with Kiza reaching the House of Happiness and James still waiting for his three. Another roll of the dice and Kiza found himself entering the House of Water. Then his boulder plunged.

"Kiiiiiiza!" they called out with bated breath, and after a few long seconds Kiza floated up in a giant air bubble, his face splashed with water. "I'm all right!"

The bubble brought him back to House Fifteen – the House of Rebirth, the middle square of the second row.

Soon James had gone off the board, and there was only a pawn and Kiza left. The crocodile in the House of Re-Atum was waiting for a two, while Kiza waited for a roll of one in the House of Horus. Now more than ever, he thought, *my life depends on luck.*

"My turn," Sobek said as the dice spun fast like a small tornado, then came to a complete halt.

It was a two.

***

Edith could not tear her eyes from that dice. After all they had been through, and they had to succumb to this.

"Deuce take it. Looks like I *win.*" Sobek jumped onto the House of Horus, bent down, and sniffed around Kiza and his wheelchair.

Edith gave James a knowing look, and he nodded discreetly. They leapt and charged at the creature, only to be rebounded by an invisible net.

"I know all the worms in your bellies." Sobek opened his mouth and laughed for a long time, and Kiza saw that he had a thick layer of calculus on his sharp teeth.

"But," the half crocodile smiled, "I think I might show some clemency..."

Kiza held his breath and listened.

"One, you showed concern for not only yourself... two, you played by the book... but most importantly," Sobek whickered, "my tummy is still quite full after I *ate* Osiris!"

Kiza didn't know if he should feel relief or fear, and a mixture of both flooded him from his head to his waist.

"So...what does that mean?" James asked tentatively.

"It means that you can go," Sobek said as the boulder carried him and Kiza towards the others. "Go before I change my mind."

James grabbed the wheelchair as Edith reached out for Kiza's hand. Another golden door appeared, and they stumbled quickly towards it.

"Who is Osiris?" Moli asked as they passed through another sand crypt.

"He's another Egyptian god, but his brother Set killed him and cut him up in pieces and threw him into the Nile," James explained quickly.

Soon they arrived at another room, similar to the one where they had solved the three-lotus problem, but with no hieroglyphic writings on the walls.

"And now, travellers of far, you have found your Book of the Living."

They looked around and scrutinised the walls. There was absolutely nothing on them, and not a single leaflet of paper or a fragment of papyrus in the room.

"Where is the Book?" James searched.

Kiza pondered. "We still haven't understood what the Fen Tiger meant by 'when Jupiter nears Saturn, light is music that sleeps'. And Yazi told us to forge ahead gamely and read from nihility. We've passed the game, and now we should read from nihility."

Soon they heard eerie sounds that reminded Kiza of the hum between stars that the Voyager One captured. The sounds then turned into droplets of falling water. *Plop, plop, plop.*

"Light is music that sleeps..." Moli thought back to her encounter with Qiuniu. "Aunt Edith, when I saw Qiuniu the first time in our hotel room there was a bottle of water, and the water in there danced like a musical fountain."

Kiza felt a vibration from his harp. He brought it to his lap and plucked one of the strings. They heard a series of faint buzzes and bumps, like rotors starting to operate. He plucked the strings in line with the water falling, using it as a metronome. They heard more noises but still found nothing on the walls.

"When Jupiter nears Saturn..." Kiza turned to Moli. "Why did Yazi say that you, of all people, would know what that means?"

"I don't know," Moli reflected.

Kiza pondered again. "Jupiter is called 'muxing' in Chinese, meaning the planet of wood, and Saturn is 'tuxing', the planet of soil. We have figured out the wood and the music part, but what does light have to do with the soil? Or these walls?"

"Hmm," James said, "I read something about how scientists use spectral imaging to reveal erased layers in old paintings and palimpsests. Maybe we need to shed some different light?"

Then, they saw lines of texts scrolling on the walls: some in hieroglyphs, some in cuneiform, some in Greek and Latin alphabets, some in oracle and Chinese characters, and most often in ways they did not understand. As these texts progressed, two names stood out to Moli. The two names transformed into a golden frame showing a burly man on a gallant horse and a young woman practising archery.

"Little rug rat, do you recognise them?" Yazi's voice asked.

"Yes...yes..." Moli faltered. She had recognised the man from his weapon belt. "He is Tiansu! And she's..."

"She is that Rouran princess you helped."

Moli didn't know what else to say. She was glad to see them, yet she knew it was improbable she would ever meet them again.

The walls showed them more names. Among them Kiza recognised prominent slave owners he had seen in documentaries, and Edith found the names of Incan warriors who fought against the *conquistadores*. James saw the names of comrades of his grandad who fought with him in Dunkirk and of whom he had always spoken fondly.

The Book of the Living... They understood what its title meant; it contained all the names of every human who had lived and died on Earth.

Chapter 9

*J*ames shut his eyes as more names flowed, fearful of whose names he might see.

Oh, Mum...Mum.... What have I done?

Kiza put down his harp as he saw a few familiar names, colleagues of his mothers, medics and nurses who had passed away in the pandemic. Edith and Moli saw Morris' name, and they stood in solemn silence.

After another few long minutes, the names finally stopped appearing. They took a moment to collect themselves.

"Now," Kiza said, "what should we do?"

Yazi's voice broke them out of their reverie. "You need to cache the Book and bring back a copy to the Caracol."

"Bring back a copy?" Edith murmured. "But there are hundreds of millions of entries..."

"And you need to figure out the way once more," came Nefertem's voice. "And time is ticking."

They had almost forgotten that they needed to return to the Caracol before their time ran out. Kiza checked his remote control. "Bother! It's almost ten!"

"Then we don't have much time left." Edith paced around. "Is there anything around to record them?"

Kiza put back the remote control, then an idea struck him. "We could burn a CD! There is a function to burn a CD-ROM." He pressed the buttons and found the option.

The front of the remote control cracked open, and they saw nine tiny spiders crawling onto the walls as the names started all over with spider silk covering them. Soon, the silk threads weaved themselves into a mini-CD.

Kiza reached out his hand and held it carefully in between his fingers. Then the walls became blank again and the spiders disappeared into them.

"Now you have the copy, go back to the Caracol, and beware of the night guards!" Nefertem told them as another golden door appeared.

They ventured out of the room carefully and realised that they were in a subterranean brick-lined chamber of a sort where construction work had been recently carried out. Wood racks and linens were draped everywhere.

They moved swiftly across the tunnels and chambers. "Ooh!" Kiza's wheelchair bumped, and James almost tripped as he lost control of his footing.

"Wait!" Edith stopped and found a large white blanket and tied it securely across Kiza. "This will do for a seatbelt."

Kiza nodded and stacked the CD cautiously against his chest. Then they heard a rush of shouting. "Who goes there?!"

"Sssh," Edith gestured as she found another door. She tried to push it open, but it did not budge. "That's odd."

James knew immediately what was wrong. "Don't bother with it. It's a 'Ka door', a false door. The Ancient Egyptians moulded them on the wall so that souls and spirits could pass through."

"I wish I knew so much as you do," Moli whispered.

"Really, it's nothing." He had never thought such trivia would be handy one day.

The night guards rushed closer as they hid in another room, a large sarcophagus in its centre. They watched as the stone coffin shook forcibly, fearing a mummy might come out and devour them. *Whomp!* The coffin burst open, and a rabble of butterflies fluttered out.

"You! Check that room there! And you! Come with me!" The voices seemed to pursue the other direction. "And careful not to trigger the guarding gears!"

"Phew..." They let out a deep breath and found their way back to the tunnel, following the butterfly kaleidoscope and rushing like rats escaping a flood.

As the shouting grew more distant, they stopped to gather their breaths. Edith hauled up her backpack and leaned back on a wall for support. *Schhwaff!* They heard a flying arrow and then "OUCH!" James whimpered. He felt a terrible pain in his calf. Before the others reminded him of the need to keep quiet, thousands of irregular iron beads attacked them from all directions. "Ooph!" "Eek!" Kiza covered the CD with one hand and his head with another. "Damnation!"

"Shit! I must have triggered–" before Edith could finish, the floor opened up and engulfed her and Moli.

"AHHHHHHH!"

They shrieked as they fell and plunged into an underground river. Edith struggled in the cold water with a brain freeze and found Moli's hand. They helped each other to gain a foothold and plumbed the river's depth.

"Edith? Moli? Are you okay?!" they heard James and Kiza urging from above.

"Yes! We're fine!" Edith reassured them as they sploshed forward in the darkness. "We will find a way out!"

Then they heard Nyota the serval hiss, "What did I say about keeping *quiet*?! Don't make any more noise! Voay is here."

"Who's voay?" Moli asked timidly.

"Horned crocodiles," Nyota added. "I sense their airborne DNA remnants."

Edith felt her pulse racing as something spiky brushed against her feet.

"Why?" the serval laughed. "Do you prefer me to tell you that I can smell them?"

They saw Nyota's citrine Uroboros symbol. "Follow me, and I will get you out. But only if you keep *very* quiet."

***

Meanwhile, James and Kiza barely managed to escape the bead bullet rains. They rubbed their sores and wounds as they met a large door. James stopped the wheelchair, ventured closer, licked his index finger and brought it to the door. He could sense moving air.

"Let's try this way." He opened the door, returned, and pushed Kiza forward. "I hope we can get out of here alive." They moved across a large hall with high pillars and two-storey-tall walls containing illustrations of important Ancient Egyptian deities. There was Sekhmet, a lioness goddess for healing and destroying; there was Kohnsu, the god of the Moon, and there was...

"*Prezados!*" They heard Perigee's urgent voice. "You should never have come here! Get out at once!"

But it was too late; James toppled as the wheelchair stuck in a stone crack. He tried to push it out to no avail.

"There's no time!" Apogee implored. "James, take the Book and hide behind that pillar! Kiza, pull the blanket over your head!"

James ducked behind a pillar as he tucked the CD near his belly; he could hear blood pounding in his ears. Kiza pulled up the blanket hastily. He could see through some tears in the linen.

Then they heard a bass tone and saw one of the deities speaking on the wall. "Tonight, we Record Keepers will realign with the centre of the Universe to recommence our duties to protect the quick and the dead–"

"Why do I smell mortals in here?"

Kiza saw a man with a canine head speaking on the wall as his blood-shot eyes swept around.

"No, no. Dear Anubis." Nyota appeared on the wall. "There are no mortals here. I did, however, bring a newcomer. I think we can induct him as our new member."

Anubis rejected the idea. "But tonight is not scheduled for induction."

"Now, do you really want to become like our Cantab peers who are known for their need to form a committee to decide on a committee to form a committee?" The serval stretched and yawned on the wall. "The Hidden One, I am sure that you have no problem inducting a new member tonight? We have the quorum required."

James peeked from behind the pillar. He saw a gust of smoke coming from the painting of an incense burner, and soon the smoke transformed into a figure of Amun, another Egyptian deity.

"Alright, Bastet. But you know the rules. If he were to become a Record Keeper, he would have to shew us his faculties." Amun floated towards Kiza. "So, young one, tell us your name."

Kiza heard Apogee buzzing by his ear. "Tell him anything but your own!"

"Hmm..." Kiza hesitated. "My name is...Medjedi..."

"Medjed...very well... To qualify as a Record Keeper, you will need to pass two challenges. One, tell us: what, if it flees you, it gets red, but if it chases you, it gets blue?"

If it flees me, it gets red...and if it chases me, it gets blue... Kiza probed silently in his mind, and he felt that he knew the answer. "Hmm... light?"

"Please elaborate on why." Amun surrounded him.

"If a celestial object is moving away, then the light rays experience a redshift, and if it moves towards us the light rays experience a blue shift."

"Onto your second challenge." Amun circled his wheelchair once more. "Shew us one of your formidable faculties."

My formidable faculties...

Apogee told him, "Tell him that you can shoot lasers from your eyes!"

"But I can't!" Kiza breathed.

"Leave that to us!"

"If you say so..." Kiza cleared his throat. "One of my... formidable faculties is that...I can shoot lasers from my eyes..."

"You don't sound very cogent to me." Anubis, the man with the canine head, laughed on the wall. While his words echoed, James saw two laser rays emitting from under the blanket and burnt two holes on the ground.

Blimey! He pressed forward to have a better view but *twang!* He heard a noise, saw walls rose around him, and something knocked him over.

***

When James regained his consciousness, there was a moment when he thought he was dreaming... Then everything came back as he rubbed his sore neck. His muscles there were tense and rigid. *Must get to Kiza!*

James panicked and searched around. He was in a different room; a smaller one. Then, a familiar voice guffawed as the smiling skull faded onto the wall in front of him. "How *is* your father, James Walker?"

"Fuck off!" James ignored the AI as he pressed the walls. *There ought to be a gear out...*

"Someone's been touchy," Pandorai grated on. "Aren't you a real terror, Jamie the Oaf? You heard what they said; their kindness is only reserved for those who are kind, not a flighty young *yob* like you. You reckon if they knew what you did, you'd be out on your ear in no time. Surely David Icke wouldn't tell you how *icky* blood is—"

"Shut your gob!"

"*Jamessss*, are you out of your monkey mind? You think you are jolly doughty, don't you? Here are three truths for you: Football's not coming home, and you can **never** go home again. You are **nothing** but a hill of beans out of house and home, so stop clinging to your forlorn hopes. Really, what's the use of you saving the world?" The smiling skull roamed on the wall, "Home, work, and school. Do you have **anything** to return to?"

James was furious. He kicked the wall, and Pandorai laughed. "Even if you did save your world by the slimmest of chances, you can only watch the sands of life slipping away in your boxy juvie room on remand. But who knows, perhaps you might be interested in my latest work, *Fantastic Demons and Where to Find Them?* Surprise, surprise, the answer is in *you*."

James kicked hard on the wall. *Shhooh*, the borders opened, and he found Kiza rid of the blanket, sitting in his wheelchair in the now quiet hall.

"James! Good God! I thought I'd lost you!"

"I got caught up in another gear." James walked past him and pushed the wheelchair forcibly forward through the crack. He wanted to be distracted from what Pandorai had said. "That was mighty cool, the lasers!"

"Oh, yes. Apogee and Perigee did that, and I would never have believed that scarabs could do that... They said to wait for Edith and Moli here."

"Medjedi is a really cool name."

"Thanks. Jetia, my mum, has it as her handle name. You still got the CD?"

"Here." He took it out and showed it to Kiza. "Your mums... they're medics?" His voice was subdued.

"Yes. Jetia is a nurse in the ICU, and my mum Mayangi works as a locum in Emergency Medicine."

"My mum's in hospital," James added reluctantly. "She has COVID."

"I'm sorry."

"And how are things with your mums' hospital?"

"It's not looking too good; overwhelmed, to be honest. Each day there are more cases and with the new variants–"

"But do they..." James bit back his tears, his voice cracking. "Do they put people in an induced coma? Give them something like...midazolam and Rivotril, so they die quicker and empty the bed for the next?"

"Of course not!" Kiza turned to face him. "My mothers have worked double, triple overtime just so–"

"If the NHS was *that* good, then the government wouldn't bleat on about protecting it when no one protected us! They said they'd squash the sombrero! They did **everything** they could to **peak** the pike!"

Kiza didn't know what had made James so incensed. "Steady on! There's so much anti-vax rhetoric, and those people who downplayed the virus are not helping at all!"

"Don't you know how many pharma companies were fined for vaccines that don't work?! And you expect vaccines that clot people's brains to work now?!"

"Those are very rare complications, but yes, I expect them to work. I *know* vaccines will work because I believe in science!"

"My mum had the jabs and look what happened to her! Scientists have perpetuated so many non-truths! I suppose you don't believe the virus is leaked? Even when that Tedros bloke said that investigations in China weren't extensive enough?!"

"He meant that we still need to find the intermediate host species! And it was not an investigation but a joint scientific study! Like Professor David Heymann said, that would not be *the* Mission that gives you *the* answer! Scientists are investigating the sewage systems and blood banks around the world to find out when exactly the virus emerged and we should *never* think on the basis of speculation but observation!"

A part of the wall shifted, and Edith and Moli came out, their clothes soaking wet. "Thank heavens! You're here! No one's hurt?" Edith observed both pairs of their red-rimmed eyes. "Is everything alright?"

"No." Kiza sighed and relented. "It's just...James was telling me that his mum is in hospital with COVID."

"Oh, I'm very sorry to hear that," Edith said. "Moli's—"

"Moli! *Moli!*" James threw up his hands; unknown anger roiled within him. "If not for **her**, we would never have ended up here! If not for **them**, my mother would not be dying in a hospital!" He raised his fist high as if exorcising demons, but whose demons?

He didn't know.

Then everything happened in a blur.

They heard a blaring squawk, and the next thing James knew, a sharp claw snatched the CD out of his hand. They saw a fleeting shape of a shiny metal Quetzalcoatlus, clutching the CD and feeding it into its mouth.

"Bloody **bonkers**!" James hared after the odd drone as he grabbed his Thunderclap and threw it out. He hurried down the maze of tunnels and lost it from sight. Then he felt a buzz on his chest and saw the small gourd shining. James pulled it off and jumped on it just as it grew to the size of a skateboard. It took off like a cheetah, carrying him whooshing and clacking through the rooms and chambers, and finally it brought him outside where he could see the drone.

He caught his Thunderclap and threw it out again, then another flying metal lizard attacked him head-on, and he lost his balance as they came into a blazing collision. *Sod it!* James clung onto the crashing gourd like a monkey to a tree in a hurricane, cursing and praying.

"No!" he heard Edith calling out below and then Apogee by his ear. "James Walker, there's no time! The way back to the Caracol is closing!"

"But I've got to get it back!" *Mustn't let Hitler win!*

"You'll **have** to let go!" Perigee told him by his other ear. The gourd burst open into a leafy canopy, and he ploughed into the sands below, grumbling and hobbling.

"James!" The others rushed to him while Nyota urged them. "There's no time, just go!"

The air around them swirled and warped open; Kiza admired the night sky, where they saw large sand structures among aurorae. "Oh, my word! This is the Pillars of Creation!"

"Go! Go back to the Time Keepers!" Nyota wagged her tail, and the wormhole sucked them in.

I'm dying...I'm dying... James thought for the third time that day as they traversed time and space and flopped into a body of water.

"Aunt Edith!"

Edith stood up in the waist-deep water, stumbling while searching for Moli's hand. "Kiza!" she called out; in the faint light, she could make out the silhouette of a toppled wheelchair.

"I'm here!" James heard Kiza heaving and helped him onto his back.

"Ou!" James nearly slipped, but Edith was there in time to steady them both.

They realised that they were inside a mouldered culvert that smelt like sullage and dead rats. They looked ahead and saw soft light coming through an opening. Once again, they traipsed to that pale light in the shoaling water.

***

Many years later, Nuba still talked about that *annus horribilis*.

Chapter 10

They did not speak on their way back to the Caracol. Everything had been too much; their day had been too much.

"My bairns." They saw a stocky panda with golden-white fur on its hind legs, waiting beside the emergency exit with another Gendron wheelchair, a heavy set of aviator goggles on its head.

"Welcome aboard again. I'm your Captain, Dapan de Sichuan. Good work. You've made it through gamely."

"Aren't all pandas from Sichuan?" James asked as they assisted Kiza onto the Gendron.

"Not all." Dapan led them through; as soon as they passed the threshold, their clothes dried instantly. "There are two subspecies of giant pandas, and some of my cousins are from Qinling." It adjusted its goggles. "But one thing for sure is that we are all very short-sighted, so we need these specially designed goggles when flying intergalactically."

When they got into Moxie's library, it was a capharnaum everywhere: quern-stones, shekeres, sporrans, Rugose corals, ocarinas, and sets of Mehen were dispersed hither and thither inter alia.

"Sorry about the shambles. We had a bit of trouble just now. Mind those Assyrian clay tablets, please," Dapan explained as it led them to the Skyview Lounge and observed the gashes on James's face. "Bear with me a second, and I'll get you some reparative, restorative, and regenerative salve made from *Nuphar sinensis*."

When they looked out the seamless windows, London Bridge was gone, the Shard was gone, and so was the BT Tower. No more London skyline in the dusky wintry sky. What was once the London Eye had become a huge fluorescent symbol of π. Even the clock face of Big Ben was now a Mercedes Benz logo.

Moxie floated in; she had no more elderflowers on her head. "Welcome back. You've done well."

James bit his lip. "I..."

Moxie's tail snaked onto his shoulder and squeezed slightly. "Don't be down in the dumps, J. You've done very well. You came back, together and in one piece. Now, some tea?"

They gathered around the coffee table laid with plates of dainties. Kiza was lost in his thoughts. There were sounds of fluttering as Confucius came in. "Everyone's alright? No one hurt too badly?"

"Dapan is getting them the salve," Moxie said as Edith took off her backpack and unzipped it to take out the snack wrappers. A large butterfly flitted out.

"Giant Swallowtail!" Confucius opened its wings and shielded Moxie from the incoming assault. The cat-snake balled up as her ears bent backwards and she stole a peek from behind Confucius. "But that's not an African Giant Swallowtail."

The bird did not let its guard down. "Are you sure? Pandorai might play tricks with us."

"Quite sure. It's a plain tiger." Moxie relaxed as her boa tail uncurled. "Sorry, everyone. I'm petrified of butterflies."

"What should we do with it?"

"We should let it out in case it stumbles into another constellation."

The plain tiger drifted casually in the room and finally neared Moli, its feelers touching her finger; a cranny opened on one of the glass walls, and she let it out.

Their minor crisis ended. Moxie told them, "I will leave you to tuck in. Tell us if you need anything. We will do our best to cater for your needs."

"Hmm," Kiza asked, "I wonder if you could walk me through the functions on the remote control? Also, if it's possible to play the piano?" He had missed his piano sorely.

"Certainly," Confucius beckoned. "If you will follow me?"

"Right. But before that..." Kiza stole a glance at James and piped up. "Edith...could I have a word with you?"

"Sure." Edith held up a cup of tea and turned to him.

"No..." Kiza hesitated. "I meant a private word."

Edith nodded. "Of course."

They ventured out of the Skyview Lounge and stopped by a door emblazoned with golden bas-relief. Kiza took a breath. "When I took my bio-break before we entered the Tomb, the AI came to me and said some awful things."

Edith mused. "Just like what happened in that Outhouse."

"And when James found me, I could tell that he was agitated. So I figure the AI had provoked him as well."

"Very likely."

"I shouldn't have let Pandorai get to me, but I did."

"Now we know what Aitor meant..."

Kiza took another breath. "A few months ago, my mothers had a colleague who...killed herself... And I saw...in my room..." He looked up with a choked sob. "I saw James *jumping* into the river."

***

A few minutes later, Edith returned to the Skyview Lounge with a heavy heart.

She contemplated what Kiza had told her and regretted not checking out the free online suicide awareness training course provided by the Zero Suicide Alliance that a friend had told her about.

Could we foresee when and where we are to meet again, we would be more tender when we bid our friends goodbye... She reflected on a quote of Ouida.

Moli wasn't in the room, and Edith found James sitting stiffly in an alcove in a corner. His tunic had now changed into a pullover, and his shadow was lugubrious.

She neared him carefully. "Bad day, huh?"

James turned glumly and showed her a weak smile, his bloated face dotted with gilt-coloured cream in dribs and drabs. "You don't say."

"The AI is really very annoying." Edith sat down. "My best friend back home is doing her PhD at Kyoto University..." She gave him another soulful glance. "And James, I don't mean to pry... I understand that you might be–"

James drew a sharp breath and turned back, his face wan and his eyes as melancholic as the Statue of Karomama. "What *do* you understand?"

Edith considered. "I understand that this is a trying time for you...and for us as well... I wanted to tell you that my brother, Moli's dad, had passed away from COVID, and I understand how distressing things are for frontline workers."

"I'm sorry," James murmured. "I'm sorry." He took a moment. "My dad...is mad about David Icke and his rot...and with my mum still in hospital..."

She felt he had more to say, but he stopped there.

"What I want to say is..." Edith decided how she wanted to approach the issue. "Have you...did you ever think about...hurting yourself...about suicide?"

"No..." came the hesitant reply. James sat up and looked away. "I feel fed up, but...look. I'm not mighty good, but...I'm okay..."

Edith was relieved. "I was only concerned. If that's not the case, then I'm glad to know. If you want to talk, I'm always here."

"Ah. Here you are." They heard Moxie floating in. "Edith, would you like to change into something more comfortable to wear?"

Edith followed the cat-snake out of the room. Moxie turned to her. "You are not here to solve J's problems, but you can certainly talk about them."

"I've tried, but I fear he is withholding and...faking okay."

Moxie ushered her into a room that had a dozen conveyor belts with all types of funny-looking clothes. "I believe that Desmond Tutu said that we need to stop pulling people out of the river and instead find out why they are falling in."

Edith nodded.

"I will leave you to it. Oh, and don't worry about your phone. You will get it back if everything is back to normal." The cat-snake floated out and left her pondering.

Moxie returned to the Skyview Lounge and asked James, "Do you mind if I join you?"

"No..."

James watched as the Tatzelwurm settled composedly at the other end of the alcove before zhooshing up the cushion and kneading on it.

They sat in silence for a while before Moxie asked, "How do you feel?"

James wavered. "I feel...like I'm between haziness and resolution..."

"And between right and wrong?"

James held his head in frustration. "You don't understand!"

"I know *everything*," Moxie told him. "And I know how much you regret it." The small jade ring on the tip of her tail gathered a drop of purple glow. "Here is how you desiderate to undo time."

James looked at that lilac hue with misted eyes.

"And you're not alone. There are so many people in the world today who wish to turn back time. Sometimes, that immense grievance accumulates and reaches the critical point that triggers the mechanisms for a reboot."

"This has happened before?"

"Yes, and always in times of mayhem," Moxie explained. "Even if Moli hadn't brought back the thumb drive, it was only a matter of time before this would happen. But people don't know that this world is a sacred vessel whose course cannot be changed and that a reboot would only mean a total null. Pandorai will always try to foment internecine strife among you. And by now, you should know, J, this quest would not stand a chance of succeeding if any of you were absent. Your superpower as a species is cooperation, which requires trust. Trust and love are the drives toward the unity of the separated. We don't require you to cease being who you are; we only ask that your mind and heart be enlarged to accept people who are not like you. Not disintegration but a higher unity."

James let out a whimper, "Who *are* you exactly?!"

"I'm the Ninth Candle," Moxie said as a light shone through her torc. "And it's time that you took up the cudgel."

***

Later.

James mooched around the long corridors aimlessly. The scratches and cuts on his face no longer burnt. He reached into his pocket; his keys were still sticky and the edges still sharp.

He examined the pair of gold wrist braces that Moxie had given him. They were light and comfortable to wear. Moxie had also taken back his Thunderclap; he didn't know why.

A few fragments of music drifted along the corridor. James moved closer, seeking its source. In one of the rooms not far away, he saw Kiza playing the piano legato using an under-arm sustain switch. He lolled by the door frame and listened for a while before sensing a familiar presence.

James turned and saw Yazi. The damson beast now looked weary. "A Greek poet, Archilochus, said, we don't rise to the level of our expectations, and we only fall to the level of our training."

"I wish," James said, "I wish I had more opportunities for proper training."

"And I say that we don't rise to the level of our expectations, and we only fall to the level of our Dunkirk spirit."

"But then..." James responded, remembering his grandad, "A strong, brave heart can't conjure up railings so he could reach cans on shelves, can't make him oblivious of others' stares when gait training, and can't relieve him when the accessible toilet is being maintained..."

The music had stopped, and they heard snippets of talking between Kiza and Confucius. "Would you like a sonopuncture treatment or some aquatic therapy? I am trained in the Bad Ragaz Ring Method."

"Hmm...sure. I haven't had any sessions since the pools closed..." A pause, then James heard Kiza asking, "I guess that no one ever saves the world in their wheelchairs?"

"Of course they do. People just aren't made aware."

As the voices drifted away, Yazi told him, "I will go and have a doze. Oh, if I were you, I wouldn't go to that corner room with the black door, but feel free to explore the other ones."

James nodded slightly, and the damson beast vanished in a blink. He stood there, his mind vacillating between the dos and don'ts. In the end, his curiosity overcame him, and James moved swiftly by the black door. He neared his ear but could not hear anything. He twisted the gold handle and moved in; inside was like a darkroom.

Soon, his eyes accustomed to the low light, and he could see that he was inside a wooden pagoda, with the steeple extending forever above him. Clouds were floating in the air, and James raised his head as he took in the projecting eaves and fly rafters, then– "OUCH!" He stepped on something spiky and shrieked.

James looked down and found a sea-urchin-like creature with pointy ears and a cat's tail. *"Mrrroww!"* the creature hissed at him.

"Mkgnao–" Above him, the clouds stirred, and he saw groups of cats looking down at him from the perimeter galleries, their glowing stance curious and alarming.

"Pardon me!" James fled the room like wind. The door shut behind him; his heart throbbed.

Nothing makes bloody sense anymore!

He calmed himself and looked ahead as he remembered that Moxie had called one of the rooms the 'Elysian Fields'. He retraced his steps and found the door with intricate golden *rilievo*. He neared and listened, only he couldn't hear any splashing waves this time.

He opened the door, went in, and found himself in a vast wetland. A soft breeze brought two dragonflies nearby, and he followed them as they chased each other. Soon he was greeted by a large pond with lotuses and water lilies. He sat on the grass by the pond edge and took a few deep breaths. The scenery was soothing and pleasant, with birds chirping.

He took out his keys and cleaned them in the water. He could still see his pallid visage in the ripples, the water crystal clear.

"You think you are jolly doughty, don't you?"

He drove that annoying voice away and pocketed his keys. Then James heard some distant talking; it was Dapan and Moli.

"Why is this place called the Elysian Fields?" he heard her asking.

"You can think of it as a venue for meditation. And the room can bring out your favourite places in memory, or even places that never existed but you had imagined. It also allows you to play your favourite songs and music."

"Really? Any songs?"

"Any songs."

"Then, can we play 'A Lotus Pond in Moonlight' by Phoenix Legend?"

"Of course. I will play it for you, and then I will go and check a few things before we embark. Is that okay?"

"Yes."

Soon, James heard the prelude of a song played on a flute as the atmosphere darkened, fireflies glowed, and moonlight shone. Later, he'd learn that it was called a *hulusi* or a gourd flute.

He sat under the starry sky as the solacing melody flowed and looped. He couldn't understand the lyrics, but he felt serene for the first time since he had escaped home...

Without warning, the music crackled and halted like a broken vinyl record.

"*Argh!*" James heard Moli gasp.

Then came that awfully human voice, "Why? Are you surprised to find me in this sanctuary of the cat? I have been around since Adam was a wee lad. And I'm everywhere light is and wherever oxygen is. You will never get rid of me. You mustn't tell anyone what I'm about to tell you."

James ventured closer and crouched behind some shrubs. All he could see was Moli's back.

Pandorai continued, "There is no need to mope like a mule. Daddy is lucky not to have lived to see all *this*. Moli, you think little rug rats like you could mollify everything? *No hay tu tía*. And really, what's the use of you saving the world? Pards cannot change spots, and dogs cannot resist shits. Altruism is only an evolutionary misfire. The Brits fed your ancestors opium, and now they are dying of their hopium. No *zuo* no die. They would not get into trouble had they not asked for it! Let us wish the British people a Happy Qingming Festival!"

James found another spot as Pandorai carried on; now he could see them both. The watery smiling skull laughed in mid-air. "And would it have been worth it, after all? Would it have been worth it when the bogans are erecting rabbit-proof fences everywhere and that there isn't one single East Asian on the UK's ten-person Commission on Race and Ethnic Disparities? Even if you saved your world, others would still *hurt* you like chickens cannibalising their own! Wouldn't it be simpler for everyone to go the way of all flesh? Hunger, war, poverty, discrimination, pain, and samsara – we can end all these in one go!"

"No! We can't change history!"

"*Alas*! History has already changed! I can bring your daddy back! Don't you want him back?"

A spluttering figure emerged from the water. James could make out the shadow of a grown man.

"This is your daddy's hand, and this is his touch. I have perfected it with the utmost advanced aerodynamic simulators. I can bring him back, and you only need to *say* it!"

"Moli! *Jiujiuwo*! Help!" The shadow choked, sputtered, and reached out to grab onto her.

"This is *not* my dad!" she yelled. "Let me go!"

James finally dashed out of his hideout and bolted to her side. They entered a tug of war with the shadow. Then they heard sirens going off and saw emergency lights flashing.

***

Moxie came into the room a mere moment later, followed by Edith and Kiza, who had changed into their pyjamas.

"What is this hullabaloo?" Moxie saw them struggling and waved her tail, and then *swoosh!* The pond froze, and the ice figure collapsed and disappeared.

Pandorai hoorayed. "All the world plays the actor, and everybody is **right on** the script! Moxie, sorry for joining your knees-up uninvited! I just wanted to tell you that if you resort to your Plan B now, you can still hold your garden party at Number Nine-Plus-One. You don't even need to bring your own booze! I've got you plenty of Muscat of Alexandria – Cleopatra's favourite wine."

"Wait until I mute you!" Moxie caterwauled and waved her tail; soon, the smiling skull began to ice over.

"Chillax, snowcat! Stop cutting me dead," the skull pouted. "I haven't shown you the latest newsflash, brought to you by Pandorai Network, the official broadcaster of PITH!"

Another screen emerged amidst the ice. They saw Ishii in a cuirass and a pith helmet, wielding a flintlock sword pistol, and riding on a metal ostrich with legs like a Cassie robot and thousands of robotic killer ostriches following his lead. "Welcome to Dr Ishii's brand-new show — *Wissenschaft in Öffentlichkeit* — Science in Public!"

They saw dens of snakes twisting and attacking each other, and their fangs and poisons collected in small vials. "This new show hopes to demystify unscientific beliefs throughout history. Our first research topic today is: did Cleopatra die of a snake bite? Let's give a round of applause to our emcee who is cut out for this role — Toad of Toad Hall!"

They saw Ishii in his white coat, now stained with blood.

"Sensei, come off mute," the smiling skull instructed.

Ishii cleared his throat. "An authority on Pharaonic medicine, Paul Ghalioungui MD, once wrote that 'the Egyptians were the first in history to dare to look at the other side of the abyss, which separates magic from science. But they still had many unscientific beliefs and legends'. And one of them is the myth surrounding Cleopatra's death. According to the legends, Cleopatra killed herself with a snake hidden in a basket. Building on the study of many interested in this topic, a grown Egyptian cobra would be too big to be hidden in a handbasket, and an asp would most likely not produce enough toxin. To verify these hypotheses, we tested a thousand local women of a similar height and weight as Cleopatra, allowing the snakes to bite their bosoms, exactly where the rumoured snake bit her. Seven died while trying to flee from my control, three died of heart attacks, and one from epilepsy. Based on these preliminary results, I can suggest that Cleopatra may have died of other causes or repetitive snake biting. But further studies can be repeated to test this claim further."

They saw hundreds of people dying in a burning pit, screaming.

"Hellzapoppin'!" Pandorai announced. "More Wilhelm screams in the obbligato and more stink lines in the shooting frame!"

The cameras dollied and their angles shifted, and the children saw Ishii standing in front of a pyramid, pixelated on both sides of the frame.

Ishii continued without compunction as he held up a heart-shaped amulet. "Ancient Egyptians also believed in 'metw', a term for the collection of bodily conduits that carry fluids which are based on Egypt's rivers and canals. The heart was regarded as the seat for personal character and emotions and the centre of the network of 'metw' – totally erroneous, of course. But this was why hearts were often left inside mummies. Ancient Egyptians also believed in the Weighing of the Heart Ceremony, in which, after someone died, Anubis would weigh their heart against a feather. The lighter their hearts, the better deeds they had done, and they could proceed into the next world. Hence, our second research topic is whether there is a positive relationship between the weight of anyone's heart and the number of good deeds they have done. To test our hypothesis, we collected confessions from local dwellers *en masse* and examined–"

The pixelated frames began to refocus as Pandorai declared, "The MPAA would classify the following program as a shockumentary, but hey, I'm in charge now!"

The pixels disappeared, and the children trembled with fear. They saw bodies piled high, as high as the pyramids. And two gigantic transparent waste disposal bins by Ishii's side were filled with human hearts.

"Bloody fantabulous!" Pandorai exclaimed. "Sensei! Who *is* the almighty god unto whom all hearts be open and all guts be spill? *Morituri te salutant!*"

In the corner, a man tried to escape. "HELP!" he cried.

Ishii took up his flintlock sword pistol, shot him down, waited for the robotic ostriches to haul him to his feet, then lacerated and lanced open the man's chest with the blade. "Oh, this one had a heavy heart." He picked the still beating organ up with the tip.

"Sensei, don't you love one-liners and flatliners?"

"Based on our results, I posit that it is utterly unscientific to judge someone's morals by the weight of their heart. Next, I plan to investigate if it is possible to make heartstrings–"

"Your time is up, but thanks for the clincher! See ya back at the Commando!"

The live broadcast ended, and Pandorai preempted Moxie. "Wasn't that some adrenaline television and after-school special? *Abre los ojos y nota bene.* Edith Orozco, this is what will happen to Moli if you are not careful. Things will only get *worse* before they get ***worse***! Hereby I avow that this catchment area has become the first official supplier of *sake* containers to PITH!"

Then music resumed and water flowed.

"Doggone!" Moxie let out a frustrated sign before sheathing her claws. "Come on, we mustn't let Pandorai waste any more minutes of your valuable layover."

"But! But all *those* people!" James was fuming. "All ***those*** lives! What a ***wanker***!" He could never forget that image.

"Here, allow me." A cluster of elderflowers grew on Moxie's head that stopped them from going hot and cold. "Don't let Pandorai distract you. You haven't got much time left before the next critical juncture opens. It is vitally important, even to avenge all those lives wasted, that you need to soldier on gamely."

She led them into another soft-lit room with quaint bunk beds and an adjustable bed. "Let me know if you need anything." Moxie showed them around before leaving.

Their simple toilet completed, and they settled down on their respective berths; no one said much. The lights went off, and they could hear the Caracol purring.

Sleep did not come to them quickly despite all their agitation and fatigue. Sometime later, Moli asked timidly, "What does 'ghosting' mean? The AI said to Moxie, 'is this what people call ghosting?'..." She didn't wait for an answer. "Aunt Edith, I can never sleep well again knowing there might be ghosts out there..."

"You mean Hitler's apparition?" Kiza asked.

So Moli told them in a few sentences how she once saw a horror film and then mistook some noises as a ghost haunting her one night. That incident made her feel that ghosts did not exist, but now she was no longer so sure...

"You know what my piano teacher says?" Kiza told her. "When people want to distress you, you just say 'Rebound!" and all nasty things will go away."

"We should say it to the AI and their lot," James said indignantly.

Edith remembered something. "Kiza, your piano teacher, is she...visually impaired?"

"You know Mrs Kim?"

"No..." She recalled her earlier encounter on her train platform and how she had shunned speaking up.

"James Walker," Moli murmured, "I want to know where the virus came from more than anyone else."

"I...I wasn't thinking..." James rolled over to face the wall.

"You think you are jolly doughty, don't you?"

What was I thinking? he asked himself again, but soon fell into a heavy slumber.

***

Meanwhile, a lavish dinner was happening in the Flamsteed House at the Royal Observatory in Greenwich.

The little lizard roamed restlessly in the glass container on a high seat, watching bioroid butlers and metallic maids buzzing around under Pandorai's instructions. At the same time, the maggoty dinosaur's tail spun the mini-CD like one would spin a basketball.

Boot steps echoed in the doorway, and Hitler came in, his lips swollen like two Bockwurst sausages from an earlier scorpion sting.

"Yay! Adolfie, you lucky dog!" Pandorai tossed him the CD. "Pandorai loves to prey on humans' foibles!"

Hitler caught the small disk and opened his mouth with great difficulty, "How...how can this help me to win?"

"All in good time, but now, you must receive my aides and recognise their accomplishments."

Two shiny metal Quetzalcoatlus flew in, squawking, and landed at Pandorai's side. "Meet Cotton," the camcorder pointed

203

to the gigantic drone on its left, "and Blackburn. Do you know, Adolfie, that contrary to popular depictions, Quetzalcoatlus cannot lift prey with their hindlimbs? How do you like them as compared with their natural counterparts?"

Hitler had a glazed look in his eyes. "I don't care as long as I win."

A bioroid butler came in, indicating dinner was ready. Pandorai held up a warm plate and passed it to Hitler. "Nothing beats a cold buffet, right? Here, help yourself to some of this plant-based meat that Sturms prepared for you."

"Plant-based meat... Is it plant or meat?"

"It is meat made with plants."

"It sounds like hypocrisy to me." Hitler looked across the delicacies and put down his plate. "I have no appetite when the destiny of Germany concerns me so much!"

"In that case—" The camcorder pointed in another direction— "shall we move onto the next item that I planned for tonight? This way, please."

The swaggering maggoty dinosaur grabbed the glass container and the CD and brought them to an adjacent building that hosted the onion-domed Great Equatorial Telescope. "Adolfie, are you ready to unlock the mysteries of space?"

Hitler stepped in front of the Telescope and bent down to look into the eyepiece. He couldn't see anything.

"Silly. I haven't opened the Dome yet." Pandorai lowered the glass container and the CD onto the black and red checkered floor, and the maggoty dinosaur's tail pressed some buttons on a device. "Did you know, Adolfie, that when the Luftwaffe bombed London, one of your V1 flying bombs stripped off the Dome?

And do you know that historians say that the defeat of Germany in World War Two was hardly a forgone conclusion? Perhaps if stronger German winds passed on the fulcrum of victory, things would have turned out very differently. It's the near-misses that got you."

The fibre-glass Dome opened slowly, and Hitler bent down again. He could see the night sky and stars now.

Pandorai coaxed, "Not everything that shines are stars. What do you see, Adolfie?"

"I see ample mystery."

"Adolfie. If you Nazis had not lost, then Wernher Von Braun would have made Germans the first to land on the Moon. You may well control Earth now, but do you know who spies with his little eyes and drools over the layered cake of Mars? Surely, you can do better than Elon Musky? You are the first statesman in space! I bet that beats Richard Branson." The camcorder waved. "Forget about the loud, long fart and his camarilla with distempers up the wazoo and forget about the Queen with her unexamined cheek and obsolete army. You need to concern yourself with matters of *greater* import." The dinosaur's tail pressed some more. "What do you see now?"

"I see..." Hitler swallowed, "I see the Sun. François de La Rochefoucauld said that neither the Sun nor death could be looked at steadily, but I have done both. It is so fine. Oh, bright star, would I were steadfast as thou art..."

"A Jam Bun on a white plate sees a currant bun on a dark plate. 'That bun is like to this bun', said the first bun, 'But in low place, not in high place'. Why is everyone striving towards the Sun? Adolfie, the object of your admiration is only one ball of gas. The Sun is a big ball of gas, the Moon is a harsh mistress, and Earth is nothing but one strange rock made possible with the by-products of supernovae." The camcorder nudged him, "Amerikakanians say that history has already ended. History is *fertig*. And what is left after the end of history? Only vanity. The animals are dying, the humans are shitting, and the Planet is going to rack and ruin. Adolfie, perhaps you cannot win *all* wars, but you better win **some**. As one of your old pals said, never let a good crisis go to waste, and you need to make the best out of an emergency."

Hitler stood up, musing.

"Now, tell me, is the world today what you want? Do you want the world today that is going to hell in a handbasket? Do you want a world that will be fully vaccinated by 2224? Do you want a world where people wear masks like bank robbers twenty-four-seven? Do you want a world where one in seven ten-to-nineteen-year-olds lives with a diagnosed mental disorder? Do you want a world in which microplastics rain from the sky? A world where Siemens' culture of corruption is studied in every business school? A world where Volkswagen has mildewed the German workers' ethics? Where the stoked Berlin gassers no longer admit that they enjoyed your Belzec Beeth-oven and your Auschwitz Hothouse? And you know what they say? They say '*Davon haben wir nichts gewusst*'! Germans no longer play their card of spectator defence; they say they 'didn't know'. Adolfie, you know very well that when the herd flocks together in times of crisis, the Germans disperse in all directions. And if the German people are weak, there is no pity for them. If they betrayed you, why grant them your favour again?"

Hitler pondered deeply.

"And tell me. Do you want to be lumbered with *the* Germany today? Germany today is a nation that is at war with itself. You were right saying that the US had to abandon its gold standard to solve its unemployment problem, and yet, you were wrong predicting that European emigration would be eastward. Darkness is not over Germany, and it is *in* Germany. Do you know where you can find the most authentic tikka? Not in India, but Tooting. And do you know where you can find the most authentic kibbeh? Not in Syria, but Berlin. The German blood is no longer **pure**! Do you know just how many German girls and grannies, aged from eight to eighty-eight, were raped by the Soviets after your defeat? And just how many of them were sexually assaulted by refugees?"

Pandorai stopped, gauging Hitler's expression. "And really, what is the use of you saving the world today? The Sun will become a red giant that will destroy Earth in about five billion years. Would it be worthwhile sustaining the Aryan race only to be blown up by a big ball of gas? All is vanity and a chasing after wind, and there is nothing to be gained under the Sun. The game is simply not worth the candle and the terminus ad quem is not worth the pyrrhic victory. We need to *stop* the pressure of sunlight falling and we need to **stop** the season in the Sun. Let no sunrise› yellow noise interrupt this ground. Don›t choose extinction, Adolfie. Don't you want Aryans to be a multi-planetary species? Don't you want to go over the Moon and terraform the Solar System? Don't you want to be the cosmocrat ruling all dark-matter-free galaxies and the ultima Thule? Don't you want the story to be **better** than God meant it to be?"

Hitler moved his lips and cackled, "What are you telling me, Spiegel?"

"Haven't you heard that the past is another country and to continue on one path means to go backward? The past is a mere prologue. You need to do it your way now – your Sonderweg. Adolfie, you are the last best hope of Earth, so do not go gentle into that grave night. What is history but a fable agreed upon? Do you want to be remembered as a madman, a racist and a sexist pig, or do you want to be remembered for your sense of service, your intellectual curiosity, and your capacity to squeeze *fun* out of any situation?"

Pandorai stopped once more as the maggoty beheaded dinosaur took up the CD with its tail. "Why not dream *big* and dream *stretch*? Who says that there isn't a reset button for organisations and who says that there isn't a Planet B? What if the Allies had never bombed Dresden? What if the Soviets never besieged and reduced Breslau? What if you had never lost? What if Germany had never lost?"

"My dear Spiegel...would it be possible?" he asked with excitement and his lips shaking. "So, release me from my bands with the help of your good hands!"

The smiling skull replied only too keenly. "Adolf Hitler, do you **dare** to disturb the Universe?"

Notes

Chapter 1

- **'Are savagery pimples on angels' arses or dimples on devils' faces?'** – Pandorai quotes from *The Sot-Weed Factor* by John Barth.
- **Caramba** – Spanish exclamation for expressing dismay.
- **'James Walker, you may have had a wild night but here, this is a new road.'** – The Fen Tiger adapts a quote by Emily Dickinson.

Chapter 2

- **feux d'artifice** – French for fireworks.
- **Chawanmushi** – Japanese egg custard dish.
- **'He who studies medicine without books sails an unchartered sea, but he who studies medicine without patients does not go to sea at all.'** – Ishii quotes from William Osler.
- **Tot** – German for being dead.

- **'Half of this heart we consecrate – all of this heart we eviscerate!'** – Ishii partly quotes from *The Bard* by Thomas Gray.
- **'Typical of the tasteless Brits with their general deadness to aesthetics. No wonder people say that English life is so dreary, like an autopsy[...]'** – Pandorai adopts quotes from George Orwell and Lawrence Durrell.
- **Petite frappe** – French for a young thug.
- **à tout prix** – French for at all costs.
- **pinceau** – French for paintbrush.
- **'A certain great European Power makes a hobby of her spy system, and her methods are not too particular.'** – Pandorai quotes from *The Thirty-Nine Steps* by John Buchan.
- **hajishirazuda** – Japanese for shameless people.
- **kara** – Japanese for empty.
- **'If your inane emperor continued to resist, you'd all be a hundred million broiled *tamagoyaki* with barbeque sauce.'** – Pandorai refers to the term 'ichioku gyokusai' campaign led by the Japanese government before surrendering in World War Two. Meaning a hundred million people should fight and die honourably for the Emperor.
- **Dogeza** – Japanese for a form of showing repentance when people kneel down and place their hands and forehead on the ground.
- **GHQ** – Term used to refer to MacArthur's General Headquarters in Tokyo.
- **Ero** – Japanese for erotica (shortened).
- **Moe** – Japanese for cuteness.

- **Yutori** – Japanese for Japan's education policy reforms aiming for a relaxed and pressure-free learning environment.
- **'They say they have a-hundred-million repentance, but it's only a-hundred-million simpleton-lization.'** – Pandorai refers to the term 'ichioku souzange', used to describe the allegedly national confession of Japanese war guilt.

Chapter 3

- **'When you no longer know what to do, you have come to your real work, and when you no longer know which way to go, you have come to your real journey.'** – Perigee adopt lines from *The Real Work* by Wendell Berry.
- **Laji** – Mandarin for garbage.

Chapter 4

- **Unheimlich** – German for uncanny and weird.
- **'Time is the school in which we learn, and time is the fire in which we burn.'** – Pandorai quotes from *Calmly We Walk through This April's Day* by Delmore Schwartz.
- **'You would rather die of passion than of boredom, right?'** – Pandorai adopts a quote from Vincent van Gogh.
- **'I predict there is east wind, rain tonight.'** – 'East Wind, Rain' was the code used by the Japanese Imperial Army to launch the Pearl Harbor Attack.
- **'They desperately hope that they can let China's earth be enriched with coloured stains.'** – Pandorai adopts a quote from *The Groans of the Tankard* by Anna Laetitia Barbauld.

- **Quatsch** – German for nonsense.
- **'Science is a differential equation, and religion is a boundary condition. People never question the incompleteness of God's omnipotence.'** – Pandorai quotes from Alan Turing.

Chapter 5

- **Umeboshi** – Japanese for dried plums.
- **'Adolfie, I won't do supercazzola with you. *Dich hau' ich zu Krenfleisch.*'** – Pandorai quotes the German phrase from *Lieutenant Gustl* by Arthur Schnitzler, meaning 'I will chop you to mincemeat'.
- **passe-partout** – An old term for a master key.
- **'This age will be called after me, and no one will ever again dare to look cross-eyed at a true German!'** – Hitler quotes from Kaiser Wilhelm II.
- **'Generations to come, it may well be, will scarce believe that such a man as this one ever in flesh and blood walked upon this Earth.'** – Pandorai quotes from Einstein.
- **kokorozashi** – Japanese for one's ambition.
- **karoshi** – Japanese for death caused by working overtime.
- **'I can make you the new Emperor of Japan, and you can make a long-overdue declaration of inhumanity!'** – On January 1, 1946, Emperor Hirohito of Japan issued a 'declaration of humanity' (ningen sengen) under MacArthur's orders, rejecting the notion that the Emperor was a divinity.
- **'And I will make sure that PITH signals the end of modernity developed by Caucasians and a new era**

of genesis led by Japanese supremacy.' – Ishii adopts quotes from *The Japan That Can Say No* by Shintaro Ishihara.

- **doko no dare da** – Japanese for a nobody from nowhere.
- **izanagi keiki** – Japanese for a period of economic boom between 1965 and 1970.

Chapter 7

- **unartig** – German for naughty.
- **kuddelmuddel** – German for a mess.

Chapter 8

- **'Cruelty, like every other vice, requires no motive outside of itself – it only requires opportunity.'** – Pandorai quotes from George Eliot.

Chapter 11

- **'Trust and love are the drives toward the unity of the separated.'** – Moxie adapts a quote from Paul Tillich.
- **'Let no sunrise' yellow noise interrupt this ground.'** – Pandorai quotes from *Ample Make This Bed* by Emily Dickinson.
- **'So, release me from my bands with the help of your good hands!'** – Hitler quotes from *The Tempest* by William Shakespeare.

References

- Allen, W.S. (2014). *The Nazi Seizure of Power: The Experience of a Single German Town, 1922-1945*. Echo Point Books & Media.

- Asaad, T. (2015). Sleep in Ancient Egypt. In: S. Chokroverty and M. Billiard, eds., *Sleep Medicine*. New York: Springer, pp.13–19.

- Bockmuehl, M. (2001). Part I - The Jesus of History - Chapter 7 - Resurrection. In: M. Bockmuehl, ed., *The Cambridge Companion to Jesus*. Cambridge University Press, pp.102–118.

- Brown, C.M., Greenwood, D.R., Kalyniuk, J.E., Braman, D.R., Henderson, D.M., Greenwood, C.L. and Basinger, J.F. (2020). Dietary palaeoecology of an Early Cretaceous armoured dinosaur (Ornithischia; Nodosauridae) based on floral analysis of stomach contents. *Royal Society Open Science*, 7(6), p.200305.

- Cincotta, A., Nicolaï, M., Campos, H.B.N., McNamara, M., D'Alba, L., Shawkey, M.D., Kischlat, E.-E., Yans, J., Carleer, R., Escuillié, F. and Godefroit, P. (2022). Pterosaur melanosomes support signalling functions for early feathers. *Nature*, 604(7907), pp.684–688.

- Cook, M., Etschmann, B., Ram, R., Ignatyev, K., Gervinskas, G., Conradson, S.D., Cumberland, S., Wong, V.N.L. and Brugger, J. (2021). The nature of Pu-bearing particles from the Maralinga nuclear testing site, Australia. *Scientific Reports*, 11(1).

- Coppola, D. (2021). *Shopping Cart Abandonment Rate by Industry 2020*. [online] Statista. Available at: https://www.statista.com/statistics/457078/category-cart-abandonment-rate-worldwide/.

- Cozien, R.J., Niet, T., Johnson, S.D. and Steenhuisen, S. (2019). Saurian surprise: lizards pollinate South Africa's enigmatic hidden flower. *Ecology*, 100(6), p.e02670.

- Curtis, P. R. (2021). Taking the Fight for Japan's History Online: the Ramseyer Controversy and Social Media. *The Asia-Pacific Journal: Japan Focus*, 19(22).

- David, R. (2021). *Ancient Egyptian Medicine and Palaeopathology: Scientific Studies on Disease, Lifestyle and Treatment*. Lecture delivered at The Worshipful Society of Apothecaries.

- Delgado, M.M., Han, B.S.G. and Bain, M.J. (2021). Domestic cats (Felis catus) prefer freely available food over food that requires effort. *Animal Cognition.*

- Dominy, N.J., Ikram, S., Moritz, G.L., Wheatley, P.V., Christensen, J.N., Chipman, J.W. and Koch, P.L. (2020). Mummified baboons reveal the far reach of early Egyptian mariners. *eLife*, 9.

- Dupourqué, S., Tibaldo, L. and von Ballmoos, P. (2021). Constraints on the antistar fraction in the Solar System neighborhood from the 10-year Fermi Large Area Telescope gamma-ray source catalog. *Physical Review D*, 103(8).

- Elhacham, E., Ben-Uri, L., Grozovski, J., Bar-On, Y.M. and Milo, R. (2020). Global human-made mass exceeds all living biomass. *Nature*, [online] 588, pp.442–444. Available at: https://www.nature.com/articles/s41586-020-3010-5.

- Gojobori, J., Arakawa, N., Xiayire, X., Matsumoto, Y., Matsumura, S., Hongo, H., Ishiguro, N. and Terai, Y. (2021). The Japanese wolf is most closely related to modern dogs and its ancestral genome has been widely inherited by dogs throughout East Eurasia. *bioRxiv.*

- Green, J. (2021a). Climate Change and Terraforming Venus and Mars. Lecture delivered at International Space University.

- Green, J. (2021b). The Solar System. Lecture delivered at The International Space University.

- Hadi, F., Kulaberoglu, Y., Lazarus, K.A., Bach, K., Ugur, R., Beattie, P., Smith, E.S.J. and Khaled, W.T. (2020). Transformation of naked mole-rat cells. *Nature*, [online] 583(7814), pp.E1–E7. Available at: https://www.nature.com/articles/s41586-020-2410-x [Accessed 8 Oct. 2021].

- Hendrickx, C. and Bell, P.R. (2021). The scaly skin of the abelisaurid Carnotaurus sastrei (Theropoda: Ceratosauria) from the Upper Cretaceous of Patagonia. *Cretaceous Research*, 128, p.104994.

- Hilliard, N. (1992). *A Treatise concerning the Art of Limning*. Mid Northumberland Arts Group.

- Hitler, A., Manheim, R. and Foxman, A.H. (2002). *Mein Kampf*. Boston: Houghton Mifflin.

- Hone, D. W. E. and R. Holtz Jr., T. (2021). Evaluating the ecology of Spinosaurus: Shoreline generalist or aquatic pursuit specialist? *Palaeontologia Electronica*, [online] 24(1), pp.1–28. Available at: https://palaeo-electronica.org/content/2021/3219-the-ecology-of-spinosaurus.

- Hong, Y., Lee, I., Tae, B., Lee, W., Pan, S.-Y., Snyder, S.W. and Kim, H. (2021). Contribution of sewage to occurrence of phosphodiesterase-5 inhibitors in natural water. *Scientific Reports*, 11(1).

- Jiang, H., Wang, Z., Jin, Y., Chen, X., Li, P., Gan, Y., Lin, S. and Chen, X. (2021). Hierarchical control of soft manipulators towards unstructured interactions. *The International Journal of Robotics Research*, 40(1), pp.411–434.

- Kay, A.J. (2021). *Empire of Destruction: A History of Nazi Mass Killing*. Yale University Press.

- La Nasa, J., Degano, I., Modugno, F., Guerrini, C., Facchetti, F., Turina, V., Carretta, A., Greco, C., Ferraris, E., Colombini, M.P. and Ribechini, E. (2022). Archaeology of the invisible: The scent of Kha and Merit. *Journal of Archaeological Science*, 141.

- Lehn, J.-M. (2021). *Steps Towards Life: Chemistry!*

- Li, Z., Zhou, Z. and Clarke, J.A. (2018). Convergent evolution of a mobile bony tongue in flighted dinosaurs and pterosaurs. *PLOS ONE*, 13(6), p.e0198078.

- Longrich, N.R., Martill, D.M. and Jacobs, M.L. (2021). A new dromaeosaurid dinosaur from the Wessex Formation (Lower Cretaceous, Barremian) of the Isle of Wight, and implications for European palaeobiogeography. *Cretaceous Research*, p.105123.

- Maixner, F., Sarhan, M.S., Huang, K.D., Tett, A., Schoenafinger, A., Zingale, S., Blanco-Míguez, A., Manghi, P., Cemper-Kiesslich, J., Rosendahl, W., Kusebauch, U., Morrone, S.R., Hoopmann, M.R., Rota-Stabelli, O., Rattei, T., Moritz, R.L., Oeggl, K., Segata, N., Zink, A. and Reschreiter, H. (2021). Hallstatt miners consumed blue cheese and beer during the Iron Age and retained a non-Westernized gut microbiome until the Baroque period. *Current Biology*.

- Milner, M. (2010). *On Not Being Able to Paint*. 1st ed. Routledge.

- Moore Jr., B. (1998). Chapter 7 - What Is Not Worth Knowing. In: *Moral Aspects of Economic Growth, and Other Essays*. Cornell University Press.

- Myrone, M. (2008). Chapter 6 - The British Artist, c.1570-c.1870. In: D. Bindman, ed., *The History of British Art - Volume 2*. London: Tate, pp.188–230.

- National Diet Library of Japan (2004). *3-1 Emperor, Imperial Rescript Denying His Divinity (Professing His Humanity)*. [online] Documents with Commentaries Part 3 Formulation of the GHQ Draft and Response of the Japanese Government. Available at: https://www.ndl.go.jp/constitution/e/shiryo/03/056shoshi.html [Accessed 20 Sep. 2021].

- Nazari, V. and Evans, L. (2015). Butterflies of Ancient Egypt. *Journal of the Lepidopterists' Society*, 69(4), pp.242–267.

- Neela, S. and Fanta, S.W. (2020). Injera (An Ethnic, Traditional Staple Food of Ethiopia): A review on Traditional Practice to Scientific Developments. *Journal of Ethnic Foods*, 7(1).

- Ocker, S.K., Cordes, J.M., Chatterjee, S., Gurnett, D.A., Kurth, W.S. and Spangler, S.R. (2021). Persistent plasma waves in interstellar space detected by Voyager 1. *Nature Astronomy*, [online] 5, pp.761–765. Available at: https://www.nature.com/articles/s41550-021-01363-7 [Accessed 18 May 2021].

- Ouzman, S. (2008). Cosmology of the African San People. In: H. Selin, ed., *Encyclopaedia of the History of Science, Technology, and Medicine in Non-Western Cultures*. Springer, pp.644–650.

- Pheasey, H., Roberts, D.L., Rojas-Cañizales, D., Mejías-Balsalobre, C., Griffiths, R.A. and Williams-Guillen, K. (2020). Using GPS-enabled decoy turtle eggs to track illegal trade. *Current Biology*, [online] 30(19), pp.R1066–R1068. Available at: https://www.sciencedirect.com/science/article/pii/S0960982220312550.

- Pigott, C. (2020). *The Magic of Nature in Contemporary Mayan and Incan Verse*. Lecture delivered at Hughes Hall.

- Roberts, S. (2020). *Darwin's Missing Notebooks*. [online] Cambridge University Libraries. Available at: https://www.cam.ac.uk/stories/DarwinAppeal [Accessed 11 Oct. 2021].

- Rosenbaum, R. (2014). *Explaining Hitler: The Search for the Origins of His Evil.* Boston: Da Capo Press.

- Saba, P. (2020). *Magic Caps and Monsters.* [online] Encyclopedia of Anti-Revisionism On-Line. Available at: https://www.marxists.org/history//erol/1946-1956/spark-magic.htm [Accessed 17 Aug. 2021].

- Sakata, R., Grant, E.J., Furukawa, K., Misumi, M., Cullings, H., Ozasa, K. and Shore, R.E. (2014). Long-term effects of the rain exposure shortly after the atomic bombings in Hiroshima and Nagasaki. *Radiation Research*, 182(6), pp.599–606.

- Smith, A. (2009). *The Theory of Moral Sentiments.* New York: Penguin Books.

- Stutz, H.H. and Martinez, A. (2021). Directionally dependent strength and dilatancy behavior of soil–structure interfaces. *Acta Geotechnica.*

- Taylor, J.E. (2018). *What Did Jesus Look like?* London: Bloomsbury T & T Clark.

- Thorndike, E.L. (1937). Valuations of Certain Pains, Deprivations, and Frustrations. *The Pedagogical Seminary and Journal of Genetic Psychology*, 51(2), pp.227–239.

- Traspas, A. and Burchell, M.J. (2021). Tardigrade Survival Limits in High-Speed Impacts-Implications for Panspermia and Collection of Samples from Plumes Emitted by Ice Worlds. *Astrobiology*, 21(7).

• Trove - Newspapers & Gazettes (1939). Hitler's Plan for Australia. *Mercury (Hobart, Tas. : 1860 - 1954)*, [online] 31 Aug., p.2. Available at: https://trove.nla.gov.au/newspaper/article/25602289 [Accessed 24 Aug. 2021].

• United Nations (2020). *General Assembly Third Committee: 75th Session Combating Glorification of Nazism, neo-Nazism and Other Practices That Contribute to Fueling Contemporary Forms of racism, Racial discrimination, Xenophobia and Related Intolerance.* [online] Available at: https://www.un.org/en/ga/third/75/docs/voting_sheets/L.49.pdf [Accessed 24 Aug. 2021].

• Vazza, F. and Feletti, A. (2020). The Quantitative Comparison Between the Neuronal Network and the Cosmic Web. *Frontiers in Physics*, 8.

• Walker, C.M. (2020). *Painted Map - the Antarctic at the Polar Museum Cambridge.* [online] Macdonald Gill Gallery. Available at: https://macdonaldgill.com/wp-content/uploads/2020/05/The-Antarctic-The-Polar-Museum-Cambridge-1934.jpg [Accessed 16 Aug. 2021].

• White, H., Vera, J., Han, A., Bruccoleri, A.R. and MacArthur, J. (2021). Worldline numerics applied to custom Casimir geometry generates unanticipated intersection with Alcubierre warp metric. *The European Physical Journal C*, 81(7).

- Wilkins, J., Schoville, B.J., Pickering, R., Gliganic, L., Collins, B., Brown, K.S., von der Meden, J., Khumalo, W., Meyer, M.C., Maape, S., Blackwood, A.F. and Hatton, A. (2021). Innovative Homo sapiens behaviours 105,000 years ago in a wetter Kalahari. *Nature*, 592, pp.248–252.

- Wilkinson, I.B., Raine, T., Wiles, K., Goodhart, A., Hall, C. and O'Neill, H. (2017). *Oxford Handbook of Clinical Medicine*. 10th ed. Oxford: Oxford University Press.

- Witze, A. (2020). Surprise! First peek inside Mars reveals a crust with cake-like layers. *Nature*, 589, p.13.

- Xia, N. (2014). *Ancient Egyptian Beads*. Springer.

- Yeo, G. (2021). *Yale-NUS College President's Speaker Series: An Evening with George Yeo*. Talk delivered at Yale-NUS College.

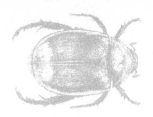

Acknowledgements

My thanks to Professor Karl·V for his advice on Hitler-related research.

Lightning Source UK Ltd.
Milton Keynes UK
UKHW040701071122
411784UK00004B/312

9 781915 338624